SOME MEMORIES, DREAMS AND REFLECTIONS

Wayne Sekulic is the author of Chasing Angels. A Dramatherapist, Teacher and Sociologist, he lives and works in the Cotswolds.

ALSO BY WAYNE SEKULIC

Chasing Angels

Some Memories, Dreams and Reflections

Wayne Sekulic

A Fairy Tale for Adults

for
Stella

Copyright © 2007 by Wayne Sekulic

ISBN 978-1-84753-797-3

Some Memories, Dreams and Reflections is a fairy tale for adults.

Set in Hampstead, London, and the Cotswolds, it's the tale of a teddy bear, Oswald, who's in Jungian Analysis, because large parts of his early memory are blank.

Oswald and his two friends, Bill and Hannah are on a quest of self-discovery.

Bill is a duck-bill platypus who turns to shamanism to combat his greatest fear - death.

Hannah is a single mum, who's trying to find meaning in her life, through a series of passionate relationships.

Some Memories, Dreams and Reflections is Oswald's tale in which we discover why large parts of his early life are like a fog. And how, through facing the shadow, our three companions save the world.

OSWALD'S TALE

Some Memories, Dreams and Reflections

Amnesia in bears is uncommon.

It often troubles Oswald that large parts of his early life history are either blank or remain extremely vague. He tells his analyst that it is like peering into a thick fog.

His analyst smiles sympathetically but doesn't respond verbally.

It is often like this when he tells his analyst such things.

Sometimes, Oswald sits face to face with him in a comfortable chair.

On other occasions he is encouraged to lie on a couch.

While on the couch Oswald often wonders what his analyst is doing because he can't see him. He has a tendency to sit behind the couch making any form of visual contact extremely difficult.

Oswald fears that all his talk will bore the old man and send him to sleep.

Often, he keeps one ear open for the sound of snoring!

Yet the analyst is a kind old man; a good listener, and very patient.

He is tall, with a large mop of silver-white hair.

Oswald has noticed that he often wears corduroy: sometimes brown and sometimes green.

His shirts are white, which offsets his bow-ties. Their floppiness and vivid colours always raise Oswald's spirits giving him a warm glowing feeling inside.

Oswald's favourites are the red, white-spotted bow-tie, which always reminds him of autumn woodlands; and the large blue floppy one, which makes him think of summer. It is cornflower-blue, his favourite colour.

Sometimes, while listening to Oswald, the analyst takes off his gold, wire-rimmed spectacles, breathes on the lenses and wipes them with his large white handkerchief. He has big pale blue eyes which twinkle when he laughs and a large bushy moustache, which trembles and quivers - mirroring his emotional response.

During these couch times, wondering if his analyst is awake, Oswald has often been tempted to sneak a look, but he never has. He feels that to do so will be cheating and will somehow betray a trust.

Today:

Oswald and the analyst sit facing each other. The sun is shining through the large window, brightening up the airy room with its book lined walls. Oswald likes books and feels that one day he might be a writer.

He's even told his analyst the same.

The old man had just nodded.

Sometimes Oswald wishes that his analyst would say more - show him some encouragement.

 He doesn't. He is just there!

Oswald's best friend, Peter, has assured him that that is what analysts do.

"Oh!" said Oswald upon receiving this revelation, going deep into himself. Often he gets lost in his own thoughts staying there for hours on end.

"What a hopeless daydreamer you are Oz," Peter says, knowing that is how he is.

Oswald loves this about Peter. He seems to understand and just accepts him.

"Warts and all!" says his analyst, smiling.

Oswald studies his paws closely looking for warts. "Yes!" he gruffles, quietly.

"What are you looking for?"

Oswald sits on his paws, "Oh, nothing," he says, lightly clearing his throat.

The old man's laughter seems to fill the room up with sunshine.

Oswald, looking bewildered but feeling happy; smiles too.

The old man waits, he knows Oswald's ways.

"I had a strange dream last night," Oswald ventures.

The analyst sits up, acknowledging Oswald's words with a nod.

Knowing the old man well, Oswald takes the nod as a cue to recount his dream.

"I'm in this beautiful green jungle. I'm a baby elephant! It's very exotic, full of wonderful sounds. Intoxicating, subtle and delicate fragrances waft on the breeze. It's my first time in the jungle and I'm very excited.

My parents are with me, plodding along, caught up in their usual banter. They have a stormy relationship and I'm often not sure why they stay together.

Choosing to ignore the tension between them I run on in front. It's my mother who calls out, "Be careful child! Stay where I can see you. I don't want you straying off the path!"

Father is absorbed in his own thoughts and unaware of my mother's concerns, content to let my mother do the worrying. Glancing back I see my mother prod my father from his reverie. "Say something to the child!" She chides. "I should hate him to wander off. Get lost in the jungle."

"Leave me to my thoughts! He'll be alright! If you worried as much over me as you do over him…, well!"

Mother frowns at my father, gives him one of her resigned sighs and allows me to continue to explore. "Mind you keep to the path!" she calls.

The jungle is powerful; its pull is intense; so bright, so fresh, so new! Curiosity and joy sweep over me, assuaging family tensions for a while. Aware of my mother's distant calls in the background, I burst through the thicket and into a clearing, and there; my eyes fall upon a large blue butterfly, sitting on a beautiful bush, its branches aflame with colour; bursting with blossoms from which the butterfly sips nectar. Never, have I seen such a wonderful, brilliant shade of blue. The butterfly's colour is bewitching! Unthinking, I rush over to it, but the noise I make scares it off. Taking flight, it makes its way deeper into the jungle. Enchanted, I follow. I do so want to touch it! To feel its blueness! But it's too wise and clever for me. Keeping itself just out of reach, it leads me deeper and deeper into he jungle. Off the path.

Lost, and tired from all the chasing, I stop to rest. In panic, I call out to my parents but there is no reply! The once bright day is now quickly fading into night.

Hungry, thirsty, scared and alone, I stand motionless in the darkness, now aware of other more scary sounds than my own rapid breathing. If only I can retrace my steps, but it's useless, I find myself going around in circles. Tired, exhausted, frightened that I will never see my parents again, hot tears fall down my cheeks. Blinded by my tears I stumble upon a watering hole. Fear and terror grip me!

"Why are you blubbing?" croaks a tree frog.

Clambering onto his bough he looks down upon me.

"I'm lost! I want my mummy and daddy!" I snuffle, trying to stem my tears.

"Come, come!" croaks the tree frog. "Big animals like you don't cry! Wipe your tears! Whatever will the jungle folk think? Such a big animal, blubbing!"

Feeling shamed, I try to quell my tears.

"Why! You're one of the biggest animals in the jungle," there's disdain in the tree frog's voice. Flicking it's long tongue it snaps up an emerald insect and pops it into its mouth. The crunching sound makes me feel a little queasy. Forlorn, tears quietly roll down my damp cheeks. To the frog, I know I must appear big and strong, but inside I am just a baby; a baby elephant, who's frightened and hungry and in need of his parents. I feel so alone! Abandoned! And very; very, unloved! Where are they!"

From the telling of his dream, powerful emotions well up inside Oswald's chest. Warm tears trickle down his furry cheeks.

The kind old man hands the little bear his large white pocket handkerchief.

Accepting it, with a pained smile, Oswald wipes his tears and gives his nose a good blow, but still they fall. Quiet sobs force their way up from the deep well in which they've been stored, waiting to bathe his long buried wounds with their salty balm.

"It's alright to cry Oswald, just let them come," the old man says gently, with compassion in his heart. He's a witness to the little bear's pain.

From a distant room, Oswald hears the chimes of an old carriage clock strike the hour. His session is over; his time up. Dabbing his eyes and giving his nose one last blow, he hands the wet hanky back to the old man who receives it with good grace.

"Thank you for sharing your dream with me Oswald, maybe we should talk about it in our next session?"

Climbing down from his chair, Oswald gives a weak smile, and nods. "I think I would like that," he says in a gruffled voice. Composing himself for the outside world, Oswald walks to the door and quietly shuts it behind him.

* * * *

Outside, in his car, Peter is waiting for him. He looks at his watch; Oswald's session is running a little late. Stuff must have come up, he thinks. He remembers his own time with the old man.

"Like the car! Austin Healey Sprite, isn't it?"

Lost in his own thoughts, Peter looks up at the smiling young woman.

"In good nick too! Did you do it up yourself?"

Peter returns the smile, "Yes! With a friend! Sorry, you caught me daydreaming…"

"She must have been a special lady," the young woman replies, aware that she'll make little headway here. She makes to move on; raising her sunglasses to the top of her head, she gives Peter a wistful smile, "You made a good job of it! I like a man who's good with his hands." And with that parting comment she continues on her way, not looking back.

"Thanks!" Peter calls out after her, and smiles, but there's a sadness in his eyes as he remembers his time with Sophie. They'd worked on the car together.

A computer whiz kid; Peter had made his first million by the age of seventeen, producing computer software for search engines.

At eighteen he'd formed his own software company with a school friend. At twenty, he'd sold his share to Itsmyne Global, a multinational, making enough money to retire for the rest of his life. Instead, he went to university and read Anthropology. He was twenty-three when he met Sophie. She was a year older than him. It was love at first sight! They'd met in Australia, both research assistants to Professor Mac Gowen, an expert on Aboriginals.

In England, they'd rented an old country house. They'd found Oswald in the nursery, looking frayed, neglected, and a little worst for ware. Sophie lovingly reinvigorated him and he quickly became an important part of their family. Everywhere they went, he went too.

In Sophie's last few weeks, he was her constant companion along with Peter. He was a great comfort to both of them. The cancer had spread rapidly and Sophie's remaining days were few. If it hadn't been for Oswald and the old man, Peter felt he might never have survived that terrible time, but life moves on and so did he.

Now it is Oswald's turn with the old man.

Peter watches him approach the car.

Oswald likes Peter's car. It is yellow and shiny and the roof comes down. Peter had even given it a name; Rupert! Oswald thinks that it might be a good name for a bear, but isn't quite sure why? When he mentioned this to his analyst, the old man had just smiled and twittered on about racial memory, whatever that meant! Trying to sound intelligent Oswald had said, "Quite so!" and sat on his paws, hoping for a change in their conversation.

Oswald climbs into his seat. Riding in Peter's car always cheers him up, especially after the sessions with his analyst.

Peter drives in silence, allowing Oswald time to collect his thoughts.

Glancing across at his furry friend, Peter gives him a reassuring smile.

"As it's such a nice day Oz, I thought we might take a stroll up on the heath, what do you say?"

"Yes!" Oswald checks his paws, just to make sure he has no unsightly growths. "What a good idea, I think I'd like that, and perhaps we could stop off at he High Street to buy an ice-cream?"

Peter laughs, "I thought you might say that."

Oswald looks at his friend expectantly, "You don't mind, do you?"

"Of course not! If you hadn't suggested it, I would have. It's just the right sort of day for an ice-cream!"

"Yes!" says Oswald, beaming all over his face.

Peter pulls up outside the ice-cream parlour and jumps out.

Oswald admires the way his friend performs this manoeuvre and wishes that he could do the same, but; alas, his legs are too short and stumpy. The last time he'd tried to perform this stunt, he remembered seeing bright stars accompanied by a stabbing pain. He'd ended up with a large lump on his head and grazes on his legs and paws.

Peter opens the door for him.

Oswald tumbles out of the car, into the parlour, stumping up to the counter - Peter in his wake. Standing on tippy-toes, Oswald tries to peer into the display cabinet.

Peter is used to this ritual, and waits for Oswald's imploring look. "Would you like me to pick you up, so that you might have a better look?"

Oswald beams, "How kind!"

Peter hoists him up.

With a clear view of all on offer, Oswald's face is a picture. Sophie had said that it was like watching the face of a holy man attaining nirvana.

A regular, Oswald is well known in the shop and is fondly referred to as "Fred", by the young staff.

Peter decides that now it is time to finally question him about this. Oswald confides that it is Marg's nickname for him.

"You mean that tall, attractive, green-eyed, tanned girl, with the Australian accent?" Peter enquires.

"Woman!" corrects Oswald.

(Peter hates it when Oswald resorts to political correctness.)

"Woman, then!" He concedes.

"Yes."

"So, what's the story?" Peter asks.

Oswald sighs. "I met her on her first day. She said she'd never served a bear before and asked me my name. I told her that I was called Oswald Theodore Threadbare and presented her with my card. She laughed and said that I sounded too swanky for her, so she'd call me Fred. I asked her what her name was. She told me Margaret. I said that if she was going to address me as Fred, then I'd call her Marg."

Oswald waits patiently as Marg serves her next customer; a tired looking lady with a baby in a sling on her chest and an aggressive, toddler tugging at her dungarees.

Seeing Oswald, Marg smiles, "Hi Fred! Who's the hunk with you?"

Peter blushes. He was out of practice when it comes to young attractive women.

Marg moves closer to Oswald, who is still studying the contents of the ice-cream cabinet.

"Whatyergoingtohavetoday, sport?" Marg reels off.

It amuses Oswald - the way Marg's antipodean sing-song voice asks him what he wants, seemingly without breath. "This is a very serious business," Oswald proclaims. Giving a nod towards his best friend, "He's called Peter, by the way."

"Nice to meet you Pete!" Marg offers her hand and Peter shakes it.

"The pleasure is mine," he replies.

Oswald clears his throat, "I think that I'd like to sample the Rum and Raison and perhaps the Coconut?"

Marg smiles and gives him a little red plastic spoon with a large dollop of Rum and Raison on it.

Like a true connoisseur, Oswald lifts the spoon to the light enjoying the colour of the contents, then, he sniffs it, and slowly places it into his mouth, savouring each melting moment. "Mmmmmmmn!" he growls and hands the little red spoon back. This time Marg offers him a blue plastic spoon with a dollop of coconut ice-cream on it. Oswald solemnly repeats the ritual.

"The usual?" Marg says.

"I think so!" Oswald replies.

"Cup or cone?"

"Cup pleases Marg."

"Two scoops?"

"Of course!"

Peter looks at Marg then back at Oswald, "But you've chosen vanilla!"

Marg laughs, "He always has vanilla!"

"It's my favourite!" Oswald exclaims.

"But…"

Oswald looks at Marg and shrugs.

Marg offers Peter a Belgian choc-ice-on-a-stick.

"My treat!" says Oswald, delving into his red backpack and

fishing out his coin purse. He hands Marg to correct change.

Taking the coins, Marg quickly glances towards Peter.

Sensing the charge between them, Oswald slips into action.

"Marg?" he enquires wistfully, "Are you free this evening?"

Dropping the coins into the till, Marg looks up at him and smiles, "You bet, why?"

"Well, 'Pete' and I, are a little starved of pleasant female company and we'd really appreciate it, if you'd do us the honour of coming and sharing some food with us tonight?"

Peter - annoyed at Oswald's Hampstead affectations, interrupts, "Oz means, will you have dinner with us?"

"What do you say?" quizzes Oswald, annoyed at Peter.

Marg strokes her neck, "Why sure! I'd like that!"

"That's settled then!" Taking a card out of his wallet, Oswald hands it to Marg, "Shall we say eight?"

"Great!" She takes the card, gives Peter another quick look and smiles. "See you at eight."

Walking towards the car, Oswald spoons the contents of the cup into his mouth, temporarily entering a state of vanilla-transcendental-bliss.

On the Heath, there are the usual crowds of dog-walkers, writers, philosophers, therapists, bored-looking au pairs with well-groomed children, artists, kite-flyers, and pretty single men looking for like-minded partners.

Oswald enjoys walking the Heath, eavesdropping on many

different snippets of conversations in the numerous tongues from around the globe.

"What's with the invite, Oz?" Peter asks placing his ice-cream stick in a nearby bin.

 Spotting an empty bench near the highest point, Oswald stomps towards it. "Come on Peter, or should I say 'Pete'?" Oswald smiles to himself, "Let's go and rest our paws on that bench, before someone else grabs it!"

Peter has to run to catch up, for although Oswald's a tubby sort of bear; when determined, he can shift at quite a pace.

Catching their breath, they sit and gaze upon London's vista.

"It's a grand view!" Oswald offers. "Especially on a clear day."

"Yeah," sighs Peter. "Kind of reassuring to see St. Paul's, amongst those towering citadels to Mammon."

"The sacred and the profane." Observes Oswald.

Peter gives Oswald a sideways glance, "Well?"

"Well what?"

"You're stalling Oswald."

"Look out!" Oswald cries ducking his head, as a kite swoops down over them.

"Sorry!" A tall youth, with his hair tied back in a ponytail, calls out to them, "I'm teaching my girlfriend the ropes!"

Taking in the large-breasted, bright-eyed, blond, snuggling up to the youth, Peter gives a weak smile. 'I bet you are!' he thinks.

Recomposing himself, Oswald mutters under his breath, "Sexist pig!"

"Spill!" Peter says turning back to Oswald.

Oswald furrows his brow and puts on his therapeutic voice, "I take it you're referring to Marg?"

Peter nods.

"Don't you like her?"

"What's not to like?"

"So, what's the problem?"

Peter gives a nervous smile and bites his bottom lip.

Oswald feels Peter's pain. He misses Sophie too, "I guess the pain will never fully go away, Peter, but Sophie wouldn't want you to mourn the rest of your life."

Tears well-up in Peter's eyes, "I know Oz, but it's hard! I miss her so much!"

Oz places his paw on Peter's hand and sighs, "Me too!" he snuffles.

Looking at each other, they hug and let the tears flow at their shared loss. It is some time before they regain their composures. Blowing their noses they sigh and smile.

"Let's do this for Sophie?" Oswald offers.

Peter gives one last blow, "For my lovely Sophie," he says.

"It's time for us to both step back into life Peter."

Peter gives a heartfelt sigh, "I know your right."

"It's what Sophie would want for the both of us."

"Thanks Oz!"

"Shall we walk on?" Oswald suggests, climbing down from the bench.

"I think we ought," Peter says, dropping a handful of soggy tissues into the bin.

Holding hands, they make their way down the hill towards the ponds. Each, deep in their own thoughts, comforted in their communion of friendship.

* * * *

It's Marg's half day. She's been looking forward to a jog in the park followed by a long cool beer.

"Have you seen my ipod, Bill?"

Bill sighs and looks up from his book. "Try the windowsill, by the kitchen door!" He offers, absentmindedly.

Marg enters the lounge dressed in her loose-fitting, pink running shorts and yellow cotton, torn, T-shirt top. "Thanks mate!" She walks over to him and pats him on the head, "What would I do without you?"

Looking up, Bill gives her a smile.

"Guess what?" she exclaims.

"You look chirpy today!" Bill returns, mischievously ignoring her question.

"Don't you want to know the reason why?" Marg pouts her lips.

"Sure! If you want to tell me."

"Bill Platypus! You can be so obtuse at times. If you were human I'd probably thump you!" She shakes her fist at him, mockingly.

"It's a good job I'm not then," he says, feigning fear, "Ornithorhynchus, that's me!"

Chuckling, he sits up straight, and puts on a serious, concerned, attentive-looking face.

"Well! Wanna know?" Marg asks again, sitting on the arm of his chair, placing her arm around his neck.

"Give it to me straight girl!"

"We've got a date!"

"What do yer mean? We've got a date?"

"We're going out to dinner!"

"Dinner!"

"Yeah! Tonight!"

"Geez! How did that happen? Who with?"

"A man and a bear."

"Well! Things are looking up; I guess? Dinner with a man and a bear. Should be interesting! The bear's not dangerous, is it?"

Marg laughs. "I don't think so."

"May I enquire where we are to dine?" Bill asks in his poshest pommy accent.

"Would you believe, just around the corner?"

"Fitz john's Avenue?"

"You got it!"

"And do this bear and man have names?"

"The man's called Peter and the bear, I call Fred." Marg beams.

"And you've designs on?"

Grabbing Bill's beak, Marg gives it a shake, "Wouldn't you like to know!"

"I thupose you fink that's thunny!" Bill says in a muffled voice.

"You asked for that, smarty-pants!"

"Aw, fair go, pleath let go of my beak!"

Marg relents, "Okay! Anyway, I can't chat to you all day. I've got a run to do."

"And a beer to down?" Bill smiles.

"What you reading?"

"Black Elk Speaks."

"I see you're still on your shaman trip."

"Yep!"

"Any luck?"

"I'm still working on it."

"Just a matter of time then?"

"Maybe…"

As Marg jogs around the Heath, she thinks about her meeting with Peter that morning. He's a beautiful man, but he has such deep, sad, sorrowful eyes.

* * * *

Peter is a good cook. He really enjoys the whole process of buying, preparing, cooking and presenting food. Oswald enjoys their culinary expeditions. He particularly likes large supermarkets. Peter prefers small specialist local shops; the baker, greengrocer, delicatessen, confectioner and open markets. Today, they're in a hurry, so it's the supermarket on the Finchley Road.

Oswald loves to people-watch. He really enjoys his sojourn in the brightly coloured store.

Standing in the front of the shopping trolley, he directs Peter along the rows of pretty coloured packages. He sees the lines of goods as living art with their profusion of colours, shapes, words and images. Most of all, he finds it fascinating to observe the antics of the humans.

He sees this as theatre; the theatre of life. The cast is huge! Constantly changing, it comes in many different shapes, colours, sizes and smells, each presenting their own Oscar award winning cameo presentations.

* * * *

He remembers the young, tall, thin, pale, saucer-eyed woman with straight, thin, fair hair. How stressed, angry and rigid she'd looked. She'd brought to mind the image of a butterfly that'd had its wings torn off. Traumatized and shocked. He watched her hover by the empty shelves waiting until an old lady or harassed mother reached up for the last tin of polish or carton of milk. Then, she would make her move; swoop, snatching the article away, just before their hands could reach it: a look of exhilaration, triumph and manic retribution on her face.

* * * *

He wonders at her pain.

* * * *

Bill waits for Marg while she gets ready. They live in a sunny top flat in Maresfield Gardens, two houses from the Freud Museum. Fitzjohn's Avenue runs parallel, joined by a small side street. It will take them five minutes to walk to their dinner engagement. This pleases Bill. He doesn't go out much, as people often stop and stare at him.

 Until he came to England he'd never felt so self-conscious about his appearance. But here! Suddenly he looks, and is made to feel different.

 Adults give him sidelong glances and children stop and point him out to their parents. It makes him feel like a freak. So he doesn't go out much, spending a lot of time on his own. During such times he often reflects on his mortality and the meaning of life. If he's honest, his mortality scares him. Bill fears his own death! What is it all about; this life? He remembers his roots and the old aboriginal back home in old Aussie, who'd introduced him to shamanism.

"Are you listening to me, Bill Platypus?" Marg calls from the shower.

Bill falls out of his reverie and smiles. "Sure, you were telling me how you met our hosts."

Marg smiles, and steps out of the shower towels herself down.

"From what you tell me, they seem decent sorts, I'm looking forward to meeting them."

Marg ruffles his head, "Good! I suggest we arrive at 8:15. We don't want to seem too eager, do we?"

They both laugh.

Bill's keeps noticing that, when Marg talks about Peter, there's a sparkle in her eyes. He's also detected a delicate change in her scent. This man has aroused a passion in her. Bill suspects that Oswald has picked up a similar scent from his best friend.

Not really keen on television, preferring a good book; Bill remembers watching a fascinating documentary about the wildlife of humans directed by Dickie Kookaburra, the famous naturalist. He'd been especially intrigued by the scenes relating to humans' mating habits. He also remembers being extremely embarrassed, as his parents were watching the programme with him. His father had lit his pipe when they'd showed the mating scenes, puffing furiously, gripping the pipe tightly in his beak, all the while wagging his slippers at the end of his feet.

Bill's mother had got up suddenly and asked if anybody fancied a brew, as she felt parched.

* * * *

Oswald and Peter live in a large three-storey house at the village end of the avenue. While many of the houses have been converted into flats, theirs remains intact.

Wealth has never impressed Bill or Marg, but Bill senses that Marg is attracted to Peter and that Peter is attracted to Marg. Their scents suggest that they are well matched.

After a pleasant dinner, Oswald gives Bill a knowing nod and invites him up to his private den.

"I think we can let their natures do the rest," Oswald suggests, as he leads Bill up the three flights of stairs to his private rooms. Patting his newfound friend on the back, Bill nods and smiles.

Oswald looks at Bill, "I'm so glad you could come."

"So am I," says Bill. "So am I."

* * * *

The old man looks up from his writing. It's well after midnight. He watches a moth flit around his desk lamp. Replacing the top of his fountain pen, he places it by his writing. He feels tired and sleepy. It's close to 1 a.m. and time he was in his bed. He is to see his first training analyst at 6 a.m. He wonders what his dear wife would have said, if she'd been around. She certainly wouldn't have allowed him to sit up till one, writing case notes in his study.

"Whatever next!" she'd have said, "I've no desire to live with an aspiring General Manager of the Universe! Come to bed and leave those notes. They will still be there for another day. Your mother didn't tell me I was marrying a saint!"

The old man smiles, as he climbs the stairs to his bed, a large tear falls from his eyes. "Ah Mini," he sighs, "How I miss you."

Tonight his sleep is fitful. He dreams that he is a large whale floating in a sea of consciousness surrounded by a deep blueness. All-seeing, all-wise, all-powerful; he's separated from the rest of the creatures of the ocean. Fearful of meeting his gaze or being in his great presence, all avoid him. He feels very alone. His love for them flows from every cell of his body. Such greatness frightens them.

Desperate in his hurt and loneliness the Great Whale aches in his isolation. He's alone in his grief. He remembers the telling of the savage death of his partner. How the harpoon hurtled into her being, exploding upon impact, flooding her body with pain. She'd writhed in agony, yet still her tormentors went on; cutting and tearing into her flesh, dragging the last breath of life from her. In her fear she'd cried out to him for help, as still alive they'd started electrocuting her, throwing her body into a series of terrifying spasms. Spent and exhausted they'd lashed her to the side of their boat, leaving her hanging to drown in slow agony.

If only he'd been near, he'd have smote the boat, smashing it to pieces with his mighty body, but he'd been on the other side of the ocean presiding at the High Council of Elders. He'd heard her distress calls; they'd wracked his body with grief and pain but he could not help her! He listened to her dying, and sang her the sacred death song handed down from generation to generation of their kind, comforting her as she let out her final breath; singing of his undying love for her and their child that would now never be born.

Lonely, he longs for another's touch. His great heart aches for communion with others. Greatness is an awful burden, a lonely cell. How long must he endure such pain?

Then they enter his dream. And suddenly, he's amazed, they're coming towards him from the depths of the deep blue ocean; a tiny dinghy, powered by a platypus and a teddy bear, each pulling at an oar, both unaware of their destination or the path that they have chosen. Bumping into the Great Whale, they turn to see their mistake. Fear and wonder grip their tiny furry bodies. But the Great Cosmic Whale is laughing, his great body filled with mirth. At last, he's not alone, contact has been made. He's been touched by a small bear and a platypus.

The old man wakes from his sleep with tears of laughter and pain pouring down his cheeks.

*　*　*　*

For months Bill has been trying to 'ride the drum' - to enter an altered state of consciousness and travel to the lower world to meet his power animals - but he's had no success. Composed and purified, he places his head on the pillow in the darkened room and puts on the CD of shamanic drumming. He regulates his breathing, taking in deep breaths. Feeling himself settle into his body, he listens to the drumming.

The slow rhythms of the shamanic drum begin to beat. He remembers the words of his teacher and lets his body become one with the slow beat of the drum, settling back, pressing his back flat against the floor, allowing the earth's energies to flow through him.

The task is clear, his intention formed. He has to enter into the lower worlds, through its long dark tunnel and take a look around. His teacher says he should visualise his favourite pastoral spot, somewhere peaceful and quiet, and imagine a large opening in it; a hole in the ground, or a cave. He must then visualise what it would be like entering that opening and follow it deep into the ground. His task is to walk or travel through the tunnel and eventually emerge, stepping out into the light of the lower world; the realm of the subconscious.

Bill has attempted to do this on many occasions without any success. Concentrating and trying to clear his mind is the problem. As hard as he tries, his mind stubbornly remains full of shopping lists, snippets of conversation, even debates as to the most appropriate pastoral scene to choose as an entrance.

Today it's going to be different, Bill's determined.

Slowly his body begins to relax, to lighten, and his mind starts to clear. The sound of the drum is taking on a different dimension, somehow speaking to a source buried deep within him. It is becoming his friend, a guide. An inner calm settles on him, his body is feeling light and floaty, and yet, something's still not right! Something's missing!

In the far distance something's calling to him. He begins to feel heavy, irritated by a trill buzzing in is ears. Damn it! He's forgotten to take the phone off the hook! Someone from the middle realm is trying to contact him.

Excited, but somewhat flustered he fumbles out of the darkened room and goes to answer the telephone.

"Battersea Dogs Home! Barker speaking! Can I help you?" Bill grins.

"Oh!" Oswald says, rather perplexed, "I must have dialled the wrong…"

"Oz! Me old mate! How are you?"

"Bill?" Oswald's confused

"No! Attila the Hound! Who'd you think it is?"

"Oswald, here!"

"Yes, Oz, I know."

"As Peter and Marg are out for the day I thought you might like to come over spend some time with me? We could have lunch in the garden and perhaps you could bring your didgeridoo over? I've always wanted to have a go on one."

"Sure! Great idea! They're spending a lot of time together, aren't they?" Bill comments.

"Cupid's struck, old boy!" Oswald sighs.

"You what, mate!"

"I think they're in love."

"Righto!"

"So, you'll come?"

"I'd love to, but you'll have to come around and help me with my didgeridoo."

"I'll be with you shortly."

"See you soon, then!"

* * * *

Creighton Halliday's on a downward curve. His girlfriend's left him and his bank-manager has summoned him to the bank.

Mrs Steelman informs him that he has a drink problem, as he relieves himself, in the early hours of the morning, on her prized sundial, situated on her lawn.

"Drink problem, schminck problem!" Creighton slurs back.

"Why! If my Harold was alive today! He'd knock you down!" she tells him.

"I don't give a tosh!" he says trying to click his finger and thumb together. "I'd pee on him too!" Giggling, he smoothes his hand against the nude, female statue's bottom, then, giving it a pat, promptly falls over the hedge into a flowerbed.

Returning indoors, Mrs Steelman utters curses under her breath, calling upon her god. "Lord! Smite down all sinners!" She demands; a sickly smile of retribution etching her angry, strained face. "Wipe them off the face of the Earth and cast them into your fiery pit!"

Turning over onto his side, Creighton settles down for a good night's sleep.

The sun is high in the morning sky when Creighton awakes.

Mrs Steelman raises her net curtains.

Creighton, feeling a damp tickling sensation in his ear, groans, "Leave it out Babs, I had a bit too much to drink last night!" He brushes his ear with his hand and a big fat slimy slug sticks to his fingers. It's then that he feels the damp, warm patch, slowly spreading along the length of his back and becomes aware of the snuffling sound of a dog that's just let a weight off its mind.

Opening his eyes, he turns his stiff neck, and sitting bolt-upright, kicks at the dog. The bright morning sun dazzles him, as fragments of the night begin to filter through the alcoholic haze. He shakes the slug off his fingers. A song thrush, whom he's convinced, seems intent on splitting his head apart with its warbling, mutes on him. Fumbling for his house keys, Creighton attempts to stand. His mouth tastes like a sailors armpit. What he sees next, is the final straw!

Struggling to his feet, he's confronted by the sight of a fluffy, stout, teddy bear, and a duck-billed platypus, wearing dark John Lennon shades, carrying a didgeridoo under their arms.

Shakily, Creighton Halliday makes his way up the steps to his front door, and with difficulty, letting himself in, takes a card from his wallet, picks up the phone and dials the number for Alcoholics Anonymous.

Mrs Steelman drops her net curtains and, raising her bony arms heavenwards, triumphantly cries out to her god with glee, "Praise the Lord!"

* * * *

After a substantial lunch, Oswald and Bill settle on a blanket on the lawn and fall into a contented sleep.

Bill dreams that he's sitting around a camp fire in the Australian outback with a group of bushmen whose bodies are painted with intricate white designs. They're singing songs about the beginning of time. Bill feels himself floating, being drawn into a deep well of darkness.

In Oswald's dream he's talking to an old American Indian who's beating a sacred drum. Oswald's been waiting for the Hampstead Hopper to take him up to the village, and complains that he's just missed three, that all came and left together in a convoy. The old Indian seems unsympathetic and continues drumming. The steady rhythm has a mesmeric quality to it, and to his surprise, Oswald finds himself standing outside a dark opening in the centre of one of his favourite haunts. He wonders where the opening's come from. It looks like a cave.

"There you are!" Bill shouts, sticking his head out of the darkness. "Do you know how long I've been here, waiting for you?"

Startled, Oswald's heart jumps into his mouth and he breaks wind.

"GEEZE!!! Did you have to let that one go?" Bill rumples his beak.

Oswald looks bashful, "I'm sorry, but you startled me."

"Well! Are you coming?"

"Where?"

"Inside, of course!"

"But…"

Before he could question anymore, Bill grabs hold of his arm and yanks him inside.

They find themselves travelling along, what seemed like, a dark tunnel. In the distance they can hear the faint beating of a drum.

Bill feels that it's a bit like travelling on the London Underground, as he's experiencing slight rocking motions as they journey.

Oswald feels as if he's actually falling deep into himself.

Both experience gentle twists and turns as they are propelled on their journeys.

It's Bill who first notices the small spot of light at the end of the tunnel. An end's in sight. The Lower Realm.

* * * *

In the Middle Realm mischief is afoot.

In the clear blue sky, a large dark cloud's massing. Lord Itsmyne rubs his hands with glee. His wicked spell is beginning to work. Slowly the cloud moves across the sun, blocking out its heat and light. Positioning itself over the sleeping friends it empties its contents down upon them.

* * * *

Rudely torn from their journeys, Bill and Oswald run for cover.

* * * *

The old analyst looks out of his study window. A raindrop trickles down the pane. As he awoke early that morning, he was greeted by a beautiful sunny day. Stirred and uplifted by his dream he's gone to his CD collection. Choosing the last present his dear wife, Minnie, gave him; 'Fierce Wisdom' by Chloe Goodchild. He plays his favourite track, 'How I Love You' and remembers their good times together.

Now; with this sudden cloudburst, something doesn't seem quite right! A cold shiver runs down his spine. He senses there's evil about and evokes the light.

Opening his study window, he lets in the day. Raising his eyes, he catches sight of a perfectly formed rainbow. Its beauty takes his breath away, filling his weary frame with awe at its majesty. He marvels at the logos of the Creator and feels humbled. Shaking his head, he smiles to himself, "What does it all mean? What is it all about; this experience we call life?"

Exhilarated and energised, he wipes the perspiration from his brow with his large white pocket handkerchief. His mind returns to his dream. Jung had told him that his dreams were a gift. Taking out his hunter, he flips open its silver lid and glances at the time. The rest of the day is his. He takes a deep breath and fills his lungs with the freshness after the downpour. The subtle fragrances of the garden, embrace his sense of smell. Sinking back into his comfortable chair, the old analyst closes his eyes and sighs, "Well, Carl, my old friend and mentor, I wonder what you'd have made of my dream?"

Stretching himself, he ponders on its meaning and falls into a peaceful sleep.

Outside, in the garden, a blackbird sings.

* * * *

Peter and Marg were planning to go into town and take in a gallery. The beautiful weather has dictated something else - a picnic. The sudden shower is a shock, leaving them soaked to the skin. Marg suggests a trip back to her place, "Let's take a shower and try out my new bed?"

Marg's directness, shocks, surprises and delights Peter, all at the same time. She's so natural, open, healthy. With butterflies in his stomach, Peter follows her lead, trying to appear casual and laid back.

Their lovemaking is beautiful and makes him cry. He tells her all about Sophie, her illness and his loss. Marg tells him about her love for an older man who'd returned to his wife. That afternoon they share their bodies and their pasts and fall in love.

* * * *

"Where did that come from, Oz?" Bill wraps himself in a towel. Oswald shakes the rain out of his fur. "I really have no idea."

Looking pensive he faces Bill, "We have to talk!"

"About the tunnel?" Bill ventures.

"You dreamt about it too?" Oswald looks astonished.

"Sure did!" Bill takes a red and white spotted hanky out of his pocket and removing his shades, wipes them dry. Replacing them back on his beak, he looks at Oswald, "If it was a dream."

"What are you suggesting?" Oswald looks perplexed.

Bill glances around the room, his voice taking on a conspiratorial tone, "I think these things would be better discussed in the privacy of your den. Come, follow me!"

Bemused, Oswald follows Bill up the three flights of stairs to his den. Together, they prepare afternoon tea, swapping their dreams while they work.

Over cucumber sandwiches, pots of Earl Grey tea, home-made malt loaf and Oswald's special deluxe rock cakes, Bill tells a now engrossed Oswald about his shamanic studies and his early morning attempt to 'ride the drum'.

"So this morning," Oswald enquires, brushing cake crumbs from his tummy onto a plate, "if I hadn't telephoned, you might have succeeded?"

Bill, tips his tea into his saucer, blows it and slurps it down in one, "Nah!" He says, wiping his beak with the back of his hand, "something was missing!"

Oswald winces at Bill's lack of etiquette. "Missing, how do you mean?"

Bill passes his cup to Oswald. "Fill 'er up mate!"

Oswald pours Bill another cup.

"D'you know! I've kinda got a taste for this stuff now. First time round, I thought it tasted like gnats piss, but I guess it sort of grows on you. Very refreshing! Very refreshing indeed."

Oswald wonders if he will ever get used to his antipodean friend's manners. He is now on his third pot of tea, Oswald wonders where he puts it all. "You were saying?"

Bill stops, thinks for a bit, and puts his cup and saucer down. He pushes his shades back onto his beak with his middle finger and settles back into his comfortable chair, "Oz!"

"Yes?"

"It strikes me."

Oswald waits.

"That's to say! I reckon you might be the missing ingredient!"

Oswald slumps back in his chair, "Me?"

Bill nods.

Oswald lets out a deep sigh, "You'd better tell me exactly what you mean."

Bill explains his theory.

* * * *

For several months the old analyst has noticed that a recurring theme seems to run through a number of his analysands' dreams. Many are bringing dreams of impending doom and disasters: floods, tidal waves, burning rainforests, hurricanes, earthquakes, and all other means of cataclysmic happenings.

Hannah is different.

Striking to look at, she is not conventially beautiful, but she certainly stands out in a crowd. Tall, about five feet nine inches, broad shoulders, with androgynous features, she has dark hair, cropped short. She has an honest open face. When she laughs her large green eyes sparkle. She's been in analysis with the old man for over a year and he's grown very fond of her, secretly enjoying her unconventional dress style, which he feel displays her intelligent, wild, independent, artistic streak.

Prone to follow her passions, she is a complex, searching woman, troubled, and often full of self doubt. A single parent, she's seeking the meaning of life through a series of intense sexual relationships with males and females. Often in her dreams, Hannah talks about the colour, pink. The old analyst sees this as a metaphor for Hannah, although he is holding back on any interpretation, preferring Hannah to make her own connections.

Her dreams often take the shape of a story.

With her eyes fixed in midspace Hannah delves deep within herself and starts to recount her dream. Her story.

"Pink likes life. It's new and feels really exciting. She likes the open spaces, the lush green fields, the sweet meadows with their wild, scented flowers. The creatures of the air and of the earth amaze her - stunning her with their beauty. Everything seems bright, alive and vital. She laughs as she crosses the babbling brook. Giggling, as the warm breeze nudges her along her way. What does it all mean?

Though, it has not always been like this! Sometimes the numbness returns and Pink remembers - him!

Sitting

Wooden

Bound in his world

She, in hers.

Then all is sadness

All is sad.

Honey wax for the candle flame

Heat to the butterfly wing

Death to their leaving

Death to their voice

Afraid to walk their fear

Fearful of making it their ally

They have no purpose

No direction

Their power is homeless

As they wander their separate ways.

Pink falls into a deep slumber.

In her dream, she sees herself travelling through dense forest.

She feels lonely, lost and frightened.

Tears begin to fall from her eyes, leaving puddles on the ground. Hearing her sobs, the sun filters its rays through the trees, catching her teardrops in its golden light; transforming each of the droplets into perfect rainbows.

Seeing them, Pink begins to laugh and her sobs subside.

Enchanted by the sound of her laughter the rainbows rush towards her, keen to hear more of the magical sounds flowing from her mouth. Such sweet music gladdens their ears. Bunching together they form a perfect sphere, radiating the colour of the beauty that is Pink.

Amazed, Pink follows the sphere as it floats into an opening.

In it stands a circle of standing stones. In their midst lies a beautiful pulsating crystal, glowing with a radiant light. "You came!" Its voice warms her lonely heart. "You heard our call! Now you must bring the others. We have need of you!"

In this moment, Pink knows that she is not alone. She's found her quest. Now, she can drink from the cup of life."

The old man waits for Hannah to come out of her trancelike state.

"Tell me about the standing stones," he says.

* * * *

"So! We're agreed then?"

"Yes, I think we can say that we both travelled along the same tunnel."

"Yeah!" Bill said, "And if it hadn't been for the downpour we'd probably have come out at he other end!"

"Possibly?"

Bill looks at Oswald, surprised. "What do you mean, possibly?"

Lost in his own thoughts, Oswald seems troubled.

Bill's about to ask him what's up when Oswald begins to speak. It's as if, he has resolved something in his own mind. Oswald fixes Bill with a stare, his manner has changed, and his voice, now purposeful, is authoritative.

Bill feels slightly uncomfortable.

"We're doing this all wrong, Bill! First, we need to locate our power spot."

"Go on!" Bill's eyes widened.

"Last night I had an extraordinary dream… well actually, it was more; a visitation. You remember I told you about that American Indian chappie?"

"The one banging the drum?"

"The very same!"

"Go on!" Bill nodded, encouragingly. "I'm listening."

"Well, he came to me last night, and gave me a sort of message."

"A sort of message?"

Oblivious to the response, Oswald grabs Bill's arm. "He also gave me several objects and showed me the correct way to 'ride the drum'. He said I'd need these objects if I am to perform the rituals correctly."

"WE!" corrected Bill.

"Sorry, if we are to perform the rituals correctly and enter the lower world. He also said that he'd come again."

Bill slumps back in his chair, amazed. "Geddaway! You're having me on!"

"I assure you, I'm not! Look! He gave me this rattle, smudge-stick and medicine pouch."

"Geez, Oz! I reckon you should feel honoured. What did he say about the medicine pouch?"

"You remember, you said, I was the missing ingredient?"

"Yeah!"

"He told me that I'd been chosen to 'walk the path of beauty.'"

"Become a shaman?"

Oswald nods. "The medicine pouch contains a few items of my personal medicine. He says that, in time, I'll add other items to my bundle."

"So, what does this medicine pouch do, Oz?"

Oswald gives a deep sigh. "He said it's a means of making connections; bringing the wearer into harmony with other levels of being, within the Great Everything."

"Streuth!" Bill gazes into Oswald's eyes. "Tell me you haven't been hitting he wacky-baccy, Oz!"

Oswald looks puzzled.

Bill smiles, playfully tapping Oswald on the shoulder. "Nah! You wouldn't… Forget I mentioned it."

Oswald rubs his shoulder.

"So what else did the old geezer tell you?"

"That before trying to enter the lower or higher worlds, it's essential that we consider, most carefully, what we wish to attain from the 'journey'. He said we should clarify our intentions by writing them down."

"I think Tonto's got a point there!" Bill looks about the room. "Where do you keep your writing stuff, Oz? I reckon we should write down everything the old cobber told you before you forget it! It would be a bit of a shitter, if we got the ritual wrong and turned ourselves into pumpkins now, wouldn't it?"

Oswald laughs.

Licking the tip of his pencil Bill looks to Oswald. "We'd better have a title, whaddahyersay, Oz?"

"Quite so!" Feeling important, Oswald starts to pace the room, his paw on his brow. He turns to Bill. "Ready?"

"Fire away Maestro!" Bill poises, pencil at the ready.

Oswald begins. "Details of techniques for entering altered states of consciousness and experiencing shamanic journeys to the upper and lower worlds, as told by an old American Indian, to Oswald Theodore Threadbare."

Scribbling away, Bill looks up from his notebook at Oswald. "Nifty little title, Oz!"

Oswald smiles, pleased with his efforts.

"Brains and Beauty! What a combination in one, so young!"

The irony's wasted on Oswald. Bill smiles.

When Oswald has finished, he looks at Bill's notes. They read as follows:

1. Clarify intentions of journey - focus on one thing at a time.

2. Light candle as if from your own inner light - the flame within you. That done, your mind space is now switched on for shamanic work.

3. Smudge yourself to cleanse your aura.

4. Smudge area around you, turning clockwise, this purifies the atmosphere and disperses any negatives.

5. Establish mind space sonically using rattle. This will establish a sonic globe which shields out disruptive and negative vibrations.

6. Be aware that the Shaman brings all things to his circle of awareness, in perfect balance and harmony, and centres himself with Love: The Great Bonding Force, which holds everything in existence together.

Oswald hands the notes back to Bill. "Excellent! You've certainly encapsulated the basics. These should jog our memories!"

"Great! Now I dunno about you, but all this brain work is making me hungry."

"Me too!" Oswald's looking pensive. "Let's go and eat!"

"What's on your mind, Oz?"

"I've been thinking about the message."

"Yeah! Me too!" Shutting the door behind them they walk up the hill towards the village. "I was wondering when you'd get around to that."

Linking arms, they fall into deep conversation.

* * * *

Dan Clutterbuck cusses under his breath as the telephone rings. He's been looking forward to tucking into a plate of his wife's beef stew and dumplings all day.

Frieda comes to the kitchen door with the message. "It's old man Pyke again!"

Dan looks up from his dinner. "The Boss?"

"That's what I told you!" Frieda looks annoyed.

"What's the silly old bugger want this time?" He forks a heap of hot stew into is mouth.

"He says, can you come and help him get the sheep moved from the big field?"

"Don't tell me they've got out again!"

"They have! He say's, they're all over the road, and Miss Gossip is threatening to sue him. Apparently, a sheep ran into her, knocking her off her bicycle and into the ditch!"

"Better go then love!" Dan gets up from the table. "Put my dinner in the oven and I'll have it later."

"I will this time, but I'll have words with old Pyke if this 'appens again! It's the third time this week, you've been called out on account of beasts getting out of that field! It won't do!"

It's taken a good hour to get the sheep moved to the lower field at the other end of the farm. A relieved looking Mr Pyke thanks Dan profusely, apologising for spoiling his evening meal, yet again.

"If you ask me, there's summat wrong with that big field, Boss." Dan offers, climbing back into is Landrover.

"What makes you say that?" Pyke's curious.

"Oh, I dunno!" Dan takes off his cap, scratches his head and replaces it again. "It's just a feeling!"

"Well something's wrong for sure; neither cows nor sheep want to be there!"

"You're right there, Boss! I've never known cows or sheep to break through a hedge like that before!"

"It's uncanny!"

"I wonder what Miss Gossip will make of it all?" Dan smiles.

Mr Pyke's face pales, "Please! Don't remind me. Well, thanks again, Dan."

Giving a final wave, Dan turns the ignition key and makes his way home.

"Well, I can't understand it." Frieda places Dan's warmed up meal on the table. "That spot have always bin such a special place; kind of, religious like, what with them stones and all."

Dan tucks into his dinner. "You're right there, lass! They've been standing there for a good few thousand years, I'll warrant."

"It don't make sense, do it?"

Some Memories, Dreams and Reflections

"It don't! Pass us the bread love, so as I can mop up this lovely gravy."

Musing, Frieda passes Dan the bread.

* * * *

Lord Itsmyne sits in his comfortable leather chair behind a vast antique walnut desk, in his huge opulent office, with its original works of art hanging on the walls, its marble floors, and Persian silk carpets.

Founder and owner of Itsmine Global Corporation (and if the financial press are to be believed, the thirteenth largest multi-national company in the world) success fits him well. He is a man used to having his own way. 'Fortune' estimates that he's one of the top hundred, richest men in the world.

He summons his personal assistant.

Henry Grabitall-Sharpe eases swiftly and silently beside Lord Itsmyne's desk, awaiting his employer's orders.

Looking up from his papers, Lord Itsmyne fixes Sharpe with an inquisitive stare. "I trust you've carried out my instructions?"

Grabitall-Sharpe gives a terse nod of his head. "Indeed, my Lord! Just as you said! The contents of the pouch have been in place for the past seven days."

"And to whom did you entrust this deed?" Itsmyne enquires, slowly pulling his desk drawer open.

Grabitall-Sharpe looks slightly nervous as Lord Itsmyne pulls a small silver gun from the drawer.

"Again, as you requested, I entrusted the task to two local villains: Messrs Bodgit and Blaggit."

Itsmyne points the gun towards his assistant.

Small beads of perspiration burst from his assistant's forehead.

Itsmyne fixes him with his eye.

 Henry Grabitall-Sharpe is now visibly scared and can't stop himself from shaking. Laughing, Itsmyne pulls the trigger. "A cigar?"

Grabitall-Sharpe lets out a maniacal nervous laugh, as he stares at the small naked flame, coming from the muzzle of the silver gun lighter. Clearing his throat he shakes his head. "No thank you sir, I don't smoke."

Itsmyne places the lighter back in the drawer and slides it shut. "Very wise Sharpe! We don't want you dying of cancer, do we?" He dismisses his minion. The door clicks shut and Sharpe is gone.

Pressing a button on his desk, the door to his office locks and large heavy blinds close, shutting out all light from the windows. Itsmyne moves towards his safe and opens it, drawing out a silver bowl and large phial, containing a clear liquid. Lighting a black candle, he places the bowl on his desk, pouring the contents of the phial into it. Chanting an incantation, he sits back in his chair, and waits.

A wisp of mist rises from the bowl and begins to form a cloud. He gazes into the mist as an image appears. Transported though the mist of time, he settles down to watch the events of the previous week unfold.

He looks upon Henry Grabitall-Sharpe, as he motors down a small Cotswold country lane, on his way to meet the villains Bodgit and Blaggit. Itsmyne chuckles as he watches the local crooks make their way to meet his personal assistant.

Grabitall-Sharpe waits for them at a crossroads, propped up against his car, smoking a fat Cuban cigar.

Itsmyne nods and smiles. Trust Sharpe to choose the village idiots to complete this task! How ridiculous they look, two middle-aged men, dressed in cycling helmets, goggles and the latest in high fashion, dazzling, bright, lycra cycling gear. Itsmyne watches as Sharpe gives them their instructions, handing over a small black velvet pouch. He revels in his silent glory and wonders if his minions would be so keen to carry out his bidding if they could see the bleak futures marked out for them. He's sure they would not! Pawns, mere pawns in his game; all of them! He delights in the guile of his Dark Masters.

Nergal has been received by its brothers… let the destruction commence!

* * * *

Curious, at the insistence of several of his analysands, that he watch a television documentary to be screened that evening; the old man switches on his television, sits back in his favourite armchair and views with interest. The programme's about the possibility of asteroids impacting on the earth.

He casts his mind back to a full page advertisement in 'The Times' that Hannah had shown him. It was directed to the Monarchy, the Pope, the President of the United States of America and the World's Governments. In the advertisement a nun had warned that the earth was in peril if it didn't change its wicked ways. She said it would be destroyed by a fireball.

Hannah's dream about the standing stones made a big impact on the old man's psyche. On several occasions he'd found himself dreaming that he was travelling down country lanes and hovering over a circle of standing stones, as if, waiting for something to happen, or someone to appear…

Hannah seems convinced that the end of the world will come on the twenty-first of December, 2011.

The old man feels there is not much that he can do about this!

When it comes, it comes!

Life has taught him that it is far better to savour the moment; enjoy being in the NOW!

He is puzzled about his flying dreams, though, especially his frequent visits to the stone circle. What are these dreams trying to tell him, what is their meaning?

Why are he and Hannah dreaming about Standing Stones? And why are they paying them nightly visits in their dreams?

Some Memories, Dreams and Reflections

* * * *

Blaggit boasts to his old mum that he is going on a night mission of the greatest importance, and if it proves successful, it means a considerable change in their circumstances. He will move her out of her council flat and buy her the dream cottage he's always promised her. With disdain on her face, she looks at him over her national health spectacles, belches and throws her empty Guinness bottle at him. Blaggit ducks. The bottle misses, bouncing off the wall. Quickly, he shuts the door behind him, his mother's harsh tones ringing in his ears, "Sod off! You waster!"

Bodgit and Blaggit pride themselves in dressing 'right' for their nefarious jaunts. On this occasion, they are attired in black polo neck sweaters, black, slacks, trainers and balaclavas. Bodgit, unlike Blaggit, has also blacked his face, making it almost impossible to see him in the dark. He waits behind the bush, with their tandem, for Blaggit to emerge from his mum's flat.

As usual, his exit from the old lady's place is rapid; echoes of scorn filling the night air. Bodgit wonders how such a big man as Blaggit can be so scared of such a little old lady. Waiting behind the bushes he hisses, "Pssst! Pssst!!"

Blaggit stops, listens, and looks about nervously. As he nears the bushes, Bodgit cycles out towards him, tapping him on the shoulder. Blaggit screams. Like an interrogator Bodgit shines his torch in Blaggit's face, "Shut up! YOU PILLOCK!! Do you want to wake up the whole neighbourhood? It's me! Bodgit!"

Dazzled by the torchlight, unable to see a thing, Blaggit walks towards the light, stumbling, he falls over the tandem, taking Bodgit who is seated on the front, with him. Picking themselves up, they brush themselves down, mount the tandem in unison and in stupefied silence, made their way towards the standing stones.

(Miss Gossip, who'd been looking out of her top bedroom window, told the vicar the following day that she'd seen a frightful apparition, a disembodied face floating down the lane at the stroke of midnight. She said it was the most ghastly sight she'd ever seen. Mrs Eelbake told her, that she'd heard, that in past times, terrible 'going-ons' had been reported as happening down that lane, if she knew what she meant! They both looked at each other and nodded. The vicar looked puzzled.)

Propping their tandem up against the hedge, Bodgit and Blaggit make their way through the gate and along the field to the perimeter, where the circle lies. It is a bright, starry night, the moon casting its pale blue light on the standing stones.

Bodgit turns to Blaggit, whose chubby, round, face beams at him with expectation.

"Well!" Bodgit demands.

Fumbling in his pocket, Blaggit hands the black velvet pouch over.

Bodgit recalls the words of their wealthy client:

"Remember! The stone has to be placed amongst the Whispering Knights. You'll find them about a quarter of a mile to the south-east of the stone circle. On no account place them amongst the Standing Stones!"

Silently, they make their way towards the Whispering Knights. The five large stones seem to beckon to them. Bodgit takes the amber stone from the velvet pouch and casts it into their midst. As the stone of Nergal falls amongst them, Blaggit is sure that he hears the stones sigh.

A single dark cloud passes over the moon, blocking out its light, bringing with the sudden darkness a chill breeze. From the midst of the Whispering Knights an eerie green light begins to glow. The two men scurry to their tandem, a cold silence descending upon the land.

* * * *

Itsmyne dismisses the vision and smiles. The two fools have carried out their task well. Unknown to them, Bodgit and Blaggit have opened the way for Nergal, Lord of the Underworld, Ruler of War, Plague, Flood and Destruction, to wreak his havoc!

* * * *

Reaching out to the Heavens, Nergal's dark power nudges a passing comet off its old course, placing it on a collision course for planet, Earth!

* * * *

After her sessions with the old analyst, Hannah likes to take a walk and eat her lunch on the Heath. Sometimes she eats at the café; sometimes she takes a picnic. Lying on the warm grass she watches the patterns of the pretty coloured kites, as they perform their aeronautical manoeuvres for their owners. A tall lithe young man, with long flaxen hair tied back in a pony-tail, catches her eye. She checks his pack, and taking in his body, gives him one of her winning smiles, making a mental note to check him out later, when her mind is not so full of dreams and symbols.

Hannah thinks back to her session, remembering the old man's alertness when she'd mentioned her dreams about the standing stones. He seemed unusually keen for her to talk about them. What she'd failed to mention was the strange, beaked, furry creature and the charming chubby teddy bear that had also entered her dreams. She'd looked up the beaked creature on the net and found out that it was a duck-billed platypus, a native of Australia.

 The crystal in her dream, had told her to 'bring the others'. But who are these others and how will she find them? Hannah felt a little guilty censoring her dreams. She'd never censored her sexual dreams, delighting in trying to shock her old analyst, wondering what he would make of her erotic escapades, but each time the old man had sat there motionless, impassive; so she could never really tell.

The question is: why did she censor this dream about the bear and the platypus? Is she afraid that she's finally lost it? Maybe she has!

Willow, Hannah's daughter, is spending the whole weekend with her father. The sudden freedom and her joy at feeling free leaves Hannah feeling guilty. She loves her daughter to pieces but it is so nice to have some time just for herself.

Rummaging in her blue Indian embroidered cotton backpack she searches for her lunch, pulling out an orange, a slice of hommity pie, some home-made carrot cake, a bottle of spring water, and her book. Laying out a small white napkin, she places her lunch down before her and carefully unwraps the hommity pie from its silver foil.

Two pretty young men walk past her, deep in conversation about Neale Donald Walsch's, 'Conversations with God'. She looks at their tight, pert, arses, and feels the old stirrings within her. A wicked smile passes her lips. Picking up her pie, she neatly, takes a small bite from it, savouring its spicy taste.

Hannah looks down at the book she's borrowed that morning from the Swiss Cottage library, and reads the title, 'Sacred Earth Sites'. Picking it up, she opens it up at random, and suddenly, there before her eyes, is a picture of the standing stones, that she knows so well from her dreams. Gasping in astonishment and recognition, she begins to choke on her pie. Hastily, she takes a sip of water. Her sacred stones actually exist! She's not going mad. Or, is she? Hannah pinches herself. This is for real! She studies the photograph more closely. It's unbelievable, and yet, there it is, the place she's visited every night in her dreams for the past few weeks, and it has a name; The Rollright Stones! Turning to the book's index, she finds three references, eagerly she turns to them, but there's very little real information, most of it touristy.

She reads:

"A prehistoric monument, The Rollright Stones is situated just north of the village of Little Rollright. A road passes between the Circle and the King Stone, marking the Oxfordshire/Warwickshire border following what was thought to have been from prehistoric times an important east-west route, high above the surrounding marshlands."

Hannah reads that the stones were first recorded in a twelfth century manuscript, an that since that time many historians have speculated about them. Local legend has it that an ambitious king, marching northwards with his army, met a witch at Rollright, who challenged him to advance seven strides, saying:

"If then Long Compton thou canst see
King of England shalt thou be."

Legend says that the King stepped forward confidently, but a slight mound still hid the village from his view. The witch continued:

"As Long Compton thou canst not see

King of England thou shalt not be.

Rise up stick and stand still stone,

For King of England thou shalt be none.

Thou and thy men hoar stones shall be.

And I myself an elden tree."

And so the petrified king stands rooted to the windswept hilltop, with the circle of soldiers, and the five Knights plotting treason behind him."

Hannah's real interest lies with the stone circle, 'The Kings Men.' She wonders who, why and when they'd been placed in that particular spot. The circle is about a hundred feet across, of some seventy-seven unhewn boulders varying from ground level to about seven feet in height. But what are they for and why is she dreaming about them?

She reads: 'Similar circles are to be found from Cornwall to the Orkneys, the most spectacular examples being Avebury and Stonehenge. Yet, nothing definite is known about their original purpose. There are those that speculate that the stones were used for religious ritual, possibly connected with astronomy and the changing seasons.'

Hannah closes the book, determined to find out more about her stones, as for moment, she'll enjoy her lunch and soak up some sun. It has been a busy morning.

* * * *

Oswald is beginning to look a little worse for wear and Bill seems preoccupied most of the time; his head buried deep in his shamanic books. Both are spending a great deal of time together shut away in Oswald's den.

Peter and Marg are getting worried about them and decide a small break in the country is just what they all need. They've rented a lovely cottage in the Cotswolds and plan to travel down with them the following week.

Bill and Oswald are in the den tucking into a late lunch.

Bill pours himself another cup of Earl Grey, "You're looking a bit ragged Oz, aren't you sleeping well?"

Oswald, having just taken a bite out of his sandwich, places his paw to his mouth, waving the other at Bill, indicating that he'll answer as soon as he's finished chewing.

Bill sits back in his chair and waits, "No hurry mate, finish yer grub."

Swallowing, Oswald wipes his chops with his paws, "Oh, I'm sleeping alright, but the dreams are coming thick and fast! To tell you the truth Bill, I'm waking up exhausted."

"Can't yer switch 'em off mate!"

"I don't think I can!"

Any more messages?"

"Sort of?"

"What do you mean, sort of?"

Well, that Indian chappie visited me again, last night."

Bill pushes himself back in his chair, "The fella with the drum?"

Oswald takes a sip of his tea, "Yes."

"Well, what did he say?"

"He told me that you must prepare yourself for a vision."

Bill moves rapidly forward in his seat again, "He said what?"

Oswald looks over his nose at Bill, "I think you heard me the first time."

"He said, 'I' was to prepare myself for a vision?" Bill's amazed.

"Yes."

"Do we know, when?"

"Very soon!"

Bill pushes himself back in his chair. "Geez!"

All Bill's chair to-ing and fro-ing has made Oswald feel quite dizzy, he places his cup of tea on a side-table, wondering if this is what sea-sickness feels like. Feeling a call of nature coming on, Oswald stands up to excuse himself.

"Where you going, Oz?"

Oswald wonders if his friend will ever develop some of the finer social graces. "To the loo, old chap."

"Yer going?" Bill looks slightly phased. "Toodleloo, then! See yer later?"

Perplexed, Oswald closes the door behind him.

Bill slumps back into his chair. Drowsy, he feels a deep sleep engulf him.

Leaving his body, he travels up into the firmament, amongst the stars, gazing down at the planet. Its simple beauty takes his breath away.

His consciousness shifts and he finds himself standing on a mountain. A large Golden Eagle flies down from the sky, dropping a seed on the dry soil before him. Rain falls from a small white fluffy cloud that just happens to be passing by, watering the seed.

From over the distant peaks the sun appears casting its rays upon the earth. Bill looks on in wonder as a beautiful heather bush sprouts before him, filling the air with its soothing fragrance.

At ease, he moves on in his dream. Now he's sitting in the centre of a large, ancient stone circle, before a beautiful radiant crystal. Its light fills him with joy and wonder. Happy, content and blissed-out, Bill feels that he could stay in this place forever.

It is not to be though. On the edge the circle, his eye catches the outline of a painted bushman standing on one leg and carrying a spear. Beckoning, the bushman points outside the circle. Reluctantly, Bill's gaze follows the bushman's directions. Peering out of the circle, he sees a large fire, a small way off from the ancient healing stones. The crystal's golden light is fading. As it diminishes, Bill makes out the silhouettes of five hunched figures. Their forms exude malevolence, filling Bill with fear, as the strength of their hatred envelops him. But this is not the worst of it! From within their midst arises a giant fanged serpent, its body glistening and shimmering in the red furnace light. Slowly turning towards Bill, the serpent transfixes him to the spot with its dark-eyed gaze. Poison drips from its fangs, as its quick forked tongue flicks towards him. Bill screams and screams as his worst nightmare stalks him…

Throwing open the door to the den, Peter, Marg and Oswald rush towards Bill. Petrified, Bill stands rigid, abject fear etched across his face.

"What's happening to him?" Marg bursts into tears seeing the terrified look, locked onto Bill's face.

Taking up his rattle, Oswald grasps his medicine bundle and slowly begins to circle around Bill, rattling over him, all the while chanting out a blessing, calling back his soul.

Peter and Marg look on in silence as Bill's body, relaxing, slumps to the floor. Picking him up, they move him to the couch. The screaming stops and slowly Bill emerges from his trance. Oswald continues with the purification ritual. Taking a bowl of spring water, he sprinkles it over his friend. Bill's whole body shudders, shedding a sigh that comes deep from within. Slowly, calm descends over Bill as his deepest fears subside. Stretching, yawning, he opens his eyes and stares at his friends. He's safe! He's home! Smiling at Oswald, he closes his eyes, falling into a deep, exhausted, dreamless sleep.

Some Memories, Dreams and Reflections

* * * *

It is the following morning and Oswald has overslept. Peter, Marg and Bill are taking breakfast in the garden. It's a hot summer's day:

"Hiyah Fred, catching up on your beauty sleep?" Marg greets him with a half-concerned look.

Looking up from his paper, Peter smiles.

Oswald gives Bill a studied look.

Bill's tucking into a huge bowl of muesli, brimming to the top with chopped apple, banana and orange; covered in fresh Greek yogurt and honey. Looking up, he gives Oswald a smile. His beak is covered with yogurt and honey. Licking it clean, he belches and greets Oswald, "Morning Oz, pull up a chair and get stuck in, mate!"

He belches a second time, even louder, "Excuse me manners, better out than in, though, eh?"

Marg laughs, "Did you sleep well, Oz?"

Climbing up onto his chair, Oswald turns to Marg, "Like the proverbial log. I dare say, yesterday's exertions had a lot to do with it!"

Bill looks up from his breakfast, "And what exertions would those be, Oz?"

Oswald glances quizzically at Bill and then exchanges looks with Peter and Marg, who shrug their shoulders.

Sensing that they are withholding something from him, Bill

looks from one to the other, "Is there something you guys aren't telling me?"

Tucking his table napkin under his chin, Oswald reaches for the toast.

Passing the toast to him, Marg quickly shakes her head.

Oswald realises that Bill has no recollection of yesterday's events and must have blanked them from his mind. In such circumstances it might be better to say nothing, so he follows Marg's lead.

"Actually, there is something we'd like to tell you, isn't there Pete?" Marg looks to Peter, whose head is buried deep in his newspaper. "Isn't there Pete?!"

Realising that someone is talking to him, Peter lowers, 'The Guardian.' "Sorry! Did you say something?"

Sensing Marg's irritation at his morning reading habits, Oswald tries to rescue the situation, "Marg was saying you have something to tell us?"

"I have?"

Marg kicks Peter under the table.

"Ouch! That hurts!"

"Did you knock yourself dear?" Marg gives him a scathing look.

Peter remembers the cottage, "Oh, yes, of course, how silly of me, I'd almost forgotten. Marg and I have taken a cottage down in the Cotswolds for a week and are wondering if you two fine fellows would like to join us?"

Oswald looks up from buttering his toast, "Splendid! What do you say, Bill?"

Trying to negotiate a heaped mound of scrambled eggs, dripping with tomato ketchup, between two rounds of buttered toast, Bill nods enthusiastically, "Good on yer, cobbers! Just the ticket!" He beaks his sandwich!

"Great! That's settled then! We'll be leaving this weekend," Marg smiles.

Oswald, trying to ignore Bill's gastronomic odyssey, asks Marg to pass the honey. Once again, Peter's lost in his morning paper.

Having negotiated the first quarter of his sandwich, Bill turns his attention to Peter. "So what's so interesting in the paper, Pete? I reckon Marg's beginning to feel a bit left out."

Marg cuts Bill a look.

Bill shrugs.

Lowering his paper, Peter apologises to the assembled, "Sorry, I didn't mean to be rude but there's a rather alarming article in the science section, about an asteroid that's heading on a collision course towards Jupiter next week."

"Yeah, I read something about that the other day," Bill chips in. "Some scientist are worried that the impact might affect us here on Earth."

Frowning, Marg bites her bottom lip.

Peter looks at her, concerned. "What's up, you look worried?"

Marg shakes her head, "It's nothing really and if I told you

you'd only laugh."

"Hey, if there's something bothering you, please share it." Peter coaxes.

Oswald places his paw on Marg's hand, nodding in agreement.

Bill puts aside the remains of his breakfast, "Come on gal! Tell us what's on your mind! If you can't tell your friends, who can you, tell?"

"Promise you won't think I'm mad!"

Peter kisses her on the top of her head, "We promise."

Marg takes a deep breath, "Okay, then! When I was a little kid, I used to get these, sort of, dreams regularly. I was surrounded by these big stones. I was alone and a bit frightened, but the stones were, well, kind of friendly. It was like they were protecting me from something bad that was outside."

"What was outside them?" Bill asks, caught up in her tale.

"That's just it Bill! I don't rightly know! All I do know is that it was very evil, and it wanted to lure me out of the protection of the circle, but I was frightened and wouldn't go. Outside the circle there were these five big dark figures. They promised me a new dolly if I came out to them, and said they'd give me nice thing to eat. I told them to go away and said that they were horrible, but they just laughed. It gives me the shudders, even now, thinking about their nasty laugh. Rather than entice me out they made me want to go deeper into the heart of the circle of stones, for there, I felt safe. They didn't give up though, and still they tried to get me to leave the protection of the circle. They told me that if I didn't move out of the circle then they'd send a fireball from out of the skies to burn me up and destroy the old stones. I screamed out to them that I didn't believe them. Their response was a mad laughter, each of them pointing skyward. I looked up! What I saw terrified me! I screamed! From out of the sky a huge fiery hurtling mass streamed across the firmament, making its way straight towards me and the circle of standing stones. I couldn't help myself; I just screamed and kept on screaming…"

Marg tightens her grip on Oswald's paw.

"What happened next?" Oswald prompts.

"Then my mother used to come into the room and wake me up."

Peter cradles her in his arms, "You said these dreams were a regular occurrence…"

Marg folds into his strong arms, "More like nightmares really."

Peter holds her tight, "When did they stop?"

Marg looks lovingly at Bill, "Funnily enough, when my mum gave me Bill, so that I'd have someone to snuggle up to at night. After that, the nightmares stopped."

With elbows resting on the table, propping up his head with his hands, Bill listens intently to Marg's tale. Aware of a change within himself, Bill finds himself slipping into a trancelike state. Noticing the change, Peter speaks quietly to him, "Are you alright Bill?"

The voice that replies is not that of Bill's! Now sitting upright in his chair, Bill's postures changes; his legs are folded under him, his palms facing outwards, his hands resting on his knees. Facing the bear, he makes his utterance, "You will find the maiden on the hill of tethered sails."

Amazed, Marg and Peter stare upon Bill's transformation. Oswald looks on with interest; he's recognised the Indian's voice. Taking out his pocket notebook, he writes the Indian's message down.

Bill's quick to come out of the trance and startled to see his three companions staring at him. Their collective attention unsettles him, "What are you all staring at?"

"Are you alright Bill?" Marg's the first to speak.

"Of course I am! Why are you all staring like that? Have I got a bogey on my beak or something?" Bill wipes his beak with his hand.

Oswald grins, "No Bill, but you have just channelled our mutual friend, Tonto."

"Geddaway Oz! You're having me on?"

"I assure you, I'm not! Ask the others."

Bill looks to Marg and Peter for an explanation.

"It would appear that Oswald knows something that we don't! And he's right when he says that you were speaking in a voice, other than your own," Peter confirms.

Marg strokes Bill's head, "These guys are right about the voice, you know! Sounded to me like one of those old Indian chiefs we used to cheer on, in all those American cowboy movies we watched when I was a kid!"

Bill looks up at Marg and the others, "I feel fine! So what did this old Indian say?"

Referring to his notebook Oswald quotes, "You will find the maiden on the hill of tethered sails!"

"What's he mean by that I wonder?" Bill asks.

Marg looks at Oswald and Bill, "I think you two fellas have got some explaining to do, don't you?"

Peter nods in agreement.

Taking his table napkin from under his chin, Oswald sits back in his chair, "I'm afraid it's a rather long story." He looks to Bill who nods ascent.

Sitting back, they let the story unfold.

* * * *

Bernard Flatpole's a bit of an odd character. So are a lot of the customers who frequent Oxford Centrals Cyber Café.

Tucking into a large creamy chocolate éclair, Kevin Clinton can't help overhearing a conversation Bernard's having with Tina, a buxom young waitress.

"So you see Tina, there's no point you waiting for your Knight in White Shining Armour. I reckon you'd best make hay while the sun shines."

Tina bends over Bernard's table revealing her deep cleavage.

She places his order in front of him, "So you reckon this comet has changed direction and is heading towards us, then?"

"Yep! I've already contacted the Ministry of Defence regarding my observations and have, just this minute, finished posting it on the net!"

Tina looks worried, "Isn't there anything we can do?"

Bernard shakes his head, "No! Not unless you believe in the power of prayer!"

"So what did the authorities say?"

"The usual bullshit! They thanked me for my concern and said they'd look into it."

Tina strikes one of her poses, jutting out her breasts, "You don't look too worried for somebody who's just witnessed a major shift in a comet's flight path! A shift you reckon is bringing it on a definite collision course towards Earth!"

Bernard drags his eyes from Tina's breasts to her face, "I could wear my underpants outside my trousers and pretend I'm Superman, if that would make you feel any better?"

Tina laughs, "You're kind of cool for a nerd sometimes Bernie!"

Bernard blushes, "I'll take that as a compliment then?"

Tina gives him one of her, 'isn't he nice in a nerdy sort of way smiles.'

"So Tina! What do you say? How about a date tonight? No expense spared and no holds barred!"

Tina looks at the impressive bulge in his crotch, and, wide-eyed;

straightens herself up, considering for a while Bernard's proposition; smiling, she nods her consent. "Pick me up at eight sharp!" she instructs him and wiggles back to the counter to serve another, ready order. All eyes are focussed on her shapely bum.

Bernard Flatpole rubs his hands with glee, "The world might be going to end," he mutters under his breath, "but I'm as sure as hell going to enjoy this big bang!"

* * * *

Kevin Clinton aka 'The Lonesome Rider', hacker extraordinaire, rushes back to his empty bed-sit and switches on his computer. It's going to be a busy night hacking into the defence ministry and NASA's computers. Eagerly he sets to work!

Kevin studies the screen print-ups to the sound of the dawn chorus. He shakes his head in disbelief and cusses under his breath, "Shit! Bernard's right! The comet is on a collision course and the bastards are not telling us!"

* * * *

The British Prime Minister picks up the security phone to the President of the U.S.A.

"Yoh! How you doing, Prime Minister?" The President seems his usual, youthful, cheery self. "What's your take on the latest developments?"

The Prime Minister slumps on his couch trying to quell the

desire to panic. He looks at the latest unread, 'Above Top Secret' Ministry of Defence document poking from under the latest copy of 'The New Musical Express'.

Placing his hand over the mouthpiece he shouts for Peter. "What do you mean? He's sorting out the Chinese shoe quotas?" he hisses to an aide. A senior advisor hurriedly whispers something into his ear. The P.M. smiles and nods approval at his advisor's suggestion, "Mr President! Good to hear from you! I was just about to call you as I'm undecided and wanted your opinion," he smirks at his stealth-buck-passing.

Flattered, the President takes the bait, "I've just come off the phone from the Russian and Chinese."

Pleased that he's back in control of the situation, the P. M. sits back and listens.

"All the scientist seem to agree! Can you believe that? It's official! The comet's definitely on a direct collision course with our planet!"

Sitting up straight, the P.M. speaks, "Crikey!"

The President continues, "It's been suggested that we go through the United Nations and put out a joint statement."

"Is there nothing we can do, Mr President?"

"Besides bending over backwards and kissing our arses goodbye? They say, no! "

"Double Crikey!!"

* * * *

"How can he be so horrible? When will he stop punishing me?" Hannah wipes back her tears. "A phone call! That's all it would take! But no, not him! The selfish bastard! Five hours I waited for my daughter, OUR DAUGHTER!! At the station. Ooohhh!!! He makes me so angry!!!"

"Do you still love him, Hannah?"

Hannah looks up at the old analyst, strain showing on her face, "I FUCKING HATE HIM!!!" her tears flow freely, streaming down her face, she falters, "Oh, I don't know, yes… the bastard! Why does he treat me like this? Why can't he forgive… be nice, just for once? Show me some consideration; concern?" she sobs into her hands, "Just be nice. Is that too much to ask?"

"How did you find out?" the analyst asks.

"He called the station, five hours late!"

"Couldn't you have called him?"

"No! He's not on the fucking phone!"

The analyst sighs, "I see."

"Do you really!" there's a harshness in Hannah's tone. "How can you know all the thoughts, feelings, fears, emotions that wracked my body while, helpless, I waited for my daughter. He could have contacted me before I left for the station, but no, not him! Fine, if he wanted to keep Willow for another week. I'm happy for him to see her, I really am! It's good that they should bond. Ooohhhh!!!" Hannah's despair resurfaces as she shakes her head from side-to-side in anger and despair, her body wracked in pain and grief. "It shouldn't have to be like his! Should it?" She looks up pleadingly at the old man, her face swollen with tears.

The old man's heart fills with compassion for her sense of loss and rage, since the death of his wife; he's been a companion to such feelings, often.

"Should it?" she says softly.

*　*　*　*

Eating his frugal lunch in silence, the old man composes himself for his next analysand, Oswald Theodore Threadbare.

He knows that he shouldn't have favourites, but he can't help the deep affection he holds for this stout, honest, little fellow.

 The doorbell rings and he goes to meet him. As always, Oswald checks the old man's bow-tie with a quick glance. He's wearing his blue floppy one. It had been a present from his beloved Mini on their fortieth wedding anniversary. He'd worn a similar bow-tie just like it on their very first date, all those years ago. She'd reminded him, as he'd opened the packet. He'd pretended not to remember, but he could recall the day as if it were yesterday. Why hadn't he felt able to tell her that? To share the pleasure that he'd felt in his heart? What was this foolish pride or fear that had prevented him from sharing his true feelings? Oh, how he wished he could do so now.

Quietly, they climb the stairs to the consulting room. He notices Oswald check his pockets, to see that he has his hanky. While he closes the door behind them, Oswald makes himself comfortable in the chair. The old man seats himself opposite and waits, in the time honoured way.

* * * *

Hannah splashes her tear-stained face with cold water attempting to make herself presentable to the outside world again. This last session has left her feeling raw inside. She still feels tearful, but is determined that she won't let her ex-partner constantly piss on her life. When she'd talked with Willow she'd seemed happy to stay with her father for another week. So who was she to interfere with her little girl's pleasure? But why did he always do this to her? Punish her and make her feel guilty?

How was it possible to hate someone so much, and yet, still have love for them? She had left him for an erotic adventure, which she had thought was love, but the man could not commit. What a fool she'd been to give up everything for a good lay! Why had she left him? Why had he married THAT WOMAN? Oh, she was nice enough, good to Willow, but… she would never understand him the way she had; the way she did.

Hannah wonders how she can manage to feel so unhappy on such a sunny day, obviously she has a gift for it. She gives an ironic smile. Looking into the mirror she laughs as she remembers the words of an old lover, "Hannah, with all your introspection, I'm fearful that you're going to lose yourself up your own arse, one of these days!"

Pinching her cheeks to bring some colour back into them, Hannah decides that she'll give the library a miss and go for a walk up on the Heath. Who knows, she might meet her young kite-man! Grinning to herself, she thinks of the many different ways she could take him to dizzy heights. He wouldn't even need his kite, just a lot of staying power and stamina. If he really wanted to fly she could take him to heights that were guaranteed to put a smile on his cute young face! With a smile on her face, she strides towards the Heath.

* * * *

Oswald had told Peter that he wouldn't need a lift after his session with the old man as he'd arranged to meet with Bill on the Heath for an afternoon picnic. "I'll enjoy the exercise," he'd said, "I'm growing a little too stout, a brisk walk will do me good!"

Peter had smiled.

* * * *

While Oswald is in his analysis, Bill has been researching stone circles at the library and is keen to share the results of his research with his friend. At first, he thought he might go to meet Oswald but then having second thoughts decides that it might be best if he lets Oswald have some space after his session. Jumping on a crowded Hopper to the Heath, Bill gazes out of the bus window taking in the scenes outside. Immediately, he is struck by a tall, dark-haired woman, who is bare foot and dressed in a striped baggy top and cut-off jeans. She's carrying a blue cotton bag. She strides out, up towards the hill. She has big, sad green eyes and an ironic smile on her face. She seems lost, in a world of her own.

Bill senses he's met her before, he wracks his brains, but, just can't remember where.

* * * *

Hannah enjoys her walk to the Heath. Stopping by an ice-cream parlour she treats herself to a lemon sorbet. Its clear, cool, keen, sharp taste lifts her out of herself and she's able to take in her environment, aware of the appreciative glances of the men and some of the women she passes by. Hannah is beginning to feel a bit better about herself.

* * * *

Sitting on top of Parliament Hill, Bill has been waiting a good half hour before he makes out Oswald's rotund figure stumping towards him. Quickly, he disposes of a large empty crisp packet, the contents of which he's just eaten.

Oswald arrives red-faced and a little out of breath.

"Gedday, Oz! A little out of breath, are we?"

"Just a bit," Oswald wheezes, slumping on the grass beside Bill. "How fares the research?"

"Not bad! Not Bad! Did you bring the liquid refreshment? I'm parched!"

Oswald nods.

Bill lays out a tablecloth and starts to unpack the food. As Oswald pulls off his backpack, extracting a carton of fresh orange juice and a large bottle of sparkling mineral water.

With their picnic laid out before them, Bill turns the peak of his baseball cap up, as Oswald tucks his table-napkin under his chin.

Looking at each other, they smile with glee, "I don't know about you, Oz, but my belly thinks my throats been cut? Let's trough it!"

Like true professionals they set about their task with gusto.

* * * *

As she approaches the hill, Hannah's eyes search the sky for signs of the young man's kite. There's a warm gentle breeze. A solitary blue kite with a yin-yang design gently soars the thermals, high above her. Hannah's heart sinks as she quickly surveys the skyline for signs of her chosen conquest, but his kite is nowhere to be seen, he's not there. Hannah checks out the local terrain and can't believe her eyes. Rubbing them, she looks again, "I must be dreaming?" she says to herself, "This can't be real!"

Seated, at the top of the hill are the teddy bear and the duckbill platypus from her dreams. Slightly unsure, she makes her way towards them.

Oswald is the first to notice her as he looks up from Bill's book.

Bill's explaining to him the importance of ley-lines, attempting to link them with certain energies found at ancient stone sites; which, he suggests, might go some way to explaining man's use of standing stones.

As Hannah approaches, the breeze drops, making the kite fall out of the sky towards them.

"Look out!" Oswald cries as the kite skims over their head's.

Ducking, Hannah slumps besides them, "That was close! Do you mind if I join you?"

Bill closes the book. "I saw you earlier today, walking towards the Heath!"

"Did you?" Hannah's pleased that he noticed her.

"It's hard to miss a pretty girl like you!"

"Why thank you, kind sir!"

"I hope you don't think me forward, but I'm sure I've met you before; trouble is I can't for the life of me think where!"

"You might be right," Hannah says and offers her hand. "I'm Hannah!"

Oswald and Bill take turns to shake her hand and introduce themselves.

Bill scratches his head, "Have we met before? I know I know you from somewhere…"

Hannah gives them a nervous smile, "I've certainly met you two before."

"But where?" they say in unison.

"In my dreams."

Oswald claps his paws and laughs, "Of course, you're the Hill Maiden we were told about!"

At last the penny has dropped, Bill's face breaks into an open smile, "Oz! Hannah's, the Hill Maiden! You're right, you clever old sausage! The kite is the tethered sail; we're sat on a hill, so it stands to reason! Hannah must be the Maiden!"

Hannah looks confused, "Sorry! I'm a bit lost. Perhaps you two could just run that by me again?"

Oswald produces a bag from his rucksack and offers Hannah an apple.

Bemused, Hannah accepts, "Thank you!"

"How about you tell us about your dream first?" Bill chips in.

"Dreams!" Hannah corrects, "At the Standing Stones…"

Bill and Oswald exchange glances.

"Hannah," Oswald enquires, "how did you know where to meet us?"

"Yeah!" says Bill.

Hannah looks at them and shrugs, "Until a few minutes ago, I didn't know you existed! You were just two characters in my dreams!"

"Then, nobody told you you'd find us here?" Bill asks.

Hannah frowns and bites her lower lip, "No."

"So what brought you to the Heath?" Oswald asks.

"I thought I might meet a guy up here who flies kites."

Some Memories, Dreams and Reflections

Oswald remembers a previous encounter with a kite and a young man while out walking with Peter, "I think I might have had an encounter with the chap…"

Excited, Hannah's heart gives a flutter, "Do you know him then?"

"No! But I had a near miss with his kite." Oswald remembers Peter's sadness.

"Why are you looking for him?" Bill's intrigued.

There's a twinkle in Hannah's eye, "No real reason, I just saw him the other day and thought he'd be a good lay!"

Bill rumples his beak and smiles while Oswald blushes.

Hannah laughs, "Have I shocked you? I'm sorry."

Bill straightens the peak of his cap, "I admire you're honesty, gal!"

Hannah laughs again, rubbing their backs with her hands; "I have shocked you, haven't I?" she looks delighted.

Recovering his composure, Oswald, looks at the back of his paws and addresses Hannah. "I think it's no accident that we've met. We were told by an old American Indian that we would meet a maiden, on the hill of tethered sails. We think that maiden is you !"

"Oz is right! Meeting up with us in your dreams just confirm it."

"You also know about the Standing Stones!" Oswald exclaims.

Hannah takes on a more serious frame of mind, "From what you've both said, it would seem that we have a lot to talk about?"

"Your place or ours?" Bill ventures.

Hannah shrugs, "I'm easy, let's talk!"

* * * *

Frieda Clutterbuck puts away her Hoover, shakes out her dusters and wonders how two adults and two small children can make such a mess in so short a time. Still, the extra cash is always useful and old man Pyke pays her well, which is more than she can say for the meagre wages he pays her Dan. The next people renting are: an affluent young man and his friends from London. Frieda hopes that they'll be tidier than the last lot.

Opening the windows to give the cottage a good airing, she sees, to her surprise, Miss Gossip being dragged along the field, face down, pulled by her two large Golden Labradors. From the expression of fear on the dogs face's she imagines that they're being chased by the 'hounds from hell', such is their speed! Frieda sticks her head out of the upstairs window and watches the scene unfold. "Let them go, Miss Gossip! Let them go!"

Miss Gossip is having none of it though! Clinging onto her dogs leads even tighter, she turns her head slightly sideways giving Frieda a faint smile, quickly turning back to her dogs, "Chinky! Chunky! Stop this minute! Do you hear me? You naughty dogs!" Her headscarf slips over her eyes as she's pulled over a cow pat. Her tenacity wavering, she finally lets go of the leads, her two dogs bounding off into the distance.

Trying not to laugh, Frieda runs out of the cottage towards the field to help, the now somewhat, dishevelled-looking Miss Gossip.

Sometime later, a more composed Miss Gossip sits at Frieda's kitchen table sipping a strong cup of sweet tea, with a dash of brandy, from Frieda's best bone china.

"I really don't know what's got into them! They've never done anything like this before! They're usually such good boys, so well behaved! I do hope they're alright!" Miss Gossip wipes a small tear from her cheek, with a rather soiled looking lace hanky.

Much to her surprise, Frieda can't help feeling sorry her. "Oh, I'm sure Chinky and Chunky will be fine. I saw them making off towards the village. I expect they'll be waiting for you at the kitchen door when you get home."

Miss Gossip takes another sip of her tea, her little finger raised in the air, "I do hope that you are right, Mrs Clutterbuck."

* * * *

Dan chuckles as Frieda tells him about Miss Gossip's escapades that day. Cutting himself another slice of Frieda's home-made bacon and onion suet pudding he turns to her with a quizzical expression on his face, "You say that she'd been walking in the direction of the stones?"

"Yes! That's what she said?" Frieda reaches for the teapot to refill Dan's mug, "She said that everything was fine 'til she came to the place where the Whispering Knights stand."

Dan offers Frieda his mug, "And then the dogs stopped and wouldn't go on?"

Frieda fills his mug, "That's right! Miss Gossip said that she tried pulling them but neither would budge; not a step further! It was then that she felt the cold breeze!"

Dan takes a sip from his mug, "A cold breeze?"

"That's what she said Dan! A cold breeze!"

"But the temperature has been in the nineties today! So where's this cold breeze come from?"

"Miss Gossip reckoned from them five stones!"

"The Whispering Knights?"

Frieda, now wide-eyed, nods.

"And the dogs turned about face and scarpered?"

"They did, dragging Miss Gossip with them."

"Why didn't the silly old biddy let them go?"

"You'd best ask Miss Gossip that Dan," Frieda begins to laugh as she remembers the scene; "She did look a sight Dan."

Dan laughs as well, "I bet she did!"

Farmer Pyke hears their laughter, as he passes the Clutterbuck's cottage, on his evening stroll. He's decided to take a walk up to the stones.

Miss Gossip has been on the phone to him, bending his ear about her two dogs, she's insistent that something in his field scared them, "And eventually, when I got home, the poor boys were waiting for me by the kitchen door. Mr Pyke, they were cowering and very afraid! I don't need to remind you that there is a public right of way across that field, I and my dogs, have a right to access, which means, Mr Pyke, being able to walk that way without being made fearful! So what are you going to do about it? I suggest; no, dare I say, demand, that you check it out!"

"Perhaps they saw a rabbit, and took chase?" Mr Pyke offered.

"Are you suggesting I don't feed my boys?"

"Of course not, Miss Gossip! I just mean…"

"Chinky and Chunky are well looked after and well fed! Are you seriously telling me that were frightened half out of their wits by a… by a RABBIT!"

"It was only a suggestion Miss Gossip, I didn't mean any offence."

"Mr Pyke, my dogs have been frightened. In my long experience as a country woman I can say confidently that chasing rabbits does not leave dogs fearful."

"Quite so, Miss Gossip. I'll look into it, right away!"

"Mind you do, Mr Pyke, mind you do!"

Opening the gate to the top field, Mr Pyke walks towards the Whispering Knights. He wonders what the dogs could have seen to make them so frightened. Of course, there was all the unrest with the livestock, suggesting that something might not be quite right.

Stopping, he stands and listens. There's no birdsong, movement of animals or signs of insects. The place seems still; deserted of all life. A cold chill makes him shudder, somehow the field seems different, up until a few weeks ago, livestock thrived there. So, what has happened to change all this? Now, it seems nothing wants to be there, birds, bees; even Miss Gossip's blessed dogs. "I wonder what's going on?" he says to himself.

A farmer all his life, Mr Pyke's has learned that animals are sensitive to Mother Earth and its forces, up until now, he's believed that the circle and stones have health-giving restorative properties, his livestock instinctively congregating near the ancient sites. Now, the fields feel, well, almost unhappy, as if they are burdened by an unwelcome presence.

Glad to leave the field and the stones, Mr Pyke walks in the direction of the holiday cottage. The folk from London should be arriving sometime tomorrow.

* * * *

The Hill Maiden is turning out to be excellent company.

"Hannah, Bill and I would really love it if you came down to the holiday cottage with us for a few days."

"Oz is right; we've checked it out with Peter and Marg."

"They'll be delighted if you could come, too!"

"You can stay as long as you like," Bill coaxes.

Oswald nods in agreement, "Please say that you'll come?"

"Where exactly is it that you're going?"

Bill hands her a brochure, "Here, see for yourself!"

Hannah's eyes widen as she reads the brochure, she looks at her two new friends, "How weird is that? You're actually renting a cottage near the Rollright Stones!"

"Kind of strange, isn't it?" Bill acknowledges.

"It's amazing! Was this planned before or after I told you about my dreams?" Hannah's curious.

"We didn't pick it, Peter and Marg did." Bill confides.

"Before we even met you." Oswald adds.

"This is truly mind-blowing. I've visited this place for the past three weeks in my dreams."

"We know!" Bill and Oswald blurt out.

"So how do you explain this?" Hannah asks.

"Strewth!" Bill rubs his beak.

"Synchronicity!" says Oswald.

Hannah and Bill turn to look at Oswald.

"Well! What do you say?" Oswald feeling uncomfortable with their stares decides to break the ice, "Will you come?"

"It all seems...meant. Yes, of course I'll come!" As an afterthought, she thanks them with well-placed kisses on their head's. "Thank you!"

Bill and Oswald let out sighs of relief, "Good!" they say in unison.

"Ever since we've put our heads together and pooled our

knowledge and experiences, I've developed a strong conviction that we may be all part of some mysterious adventure that's slowly beginning to unfold." Hannah says.

Bill and Oswald embrace each other tightly and gulp. "You could be right!" they blurt out rapidly.

Hannah laughs at all the drama, "If it's okay with you two, I'll come down after the weekend on the train? Perhaps you could pick me up from the station?"

Still clutching each other Oswald and Bill smile.

"If you can disentangle yourselves from each other before then, I'll meet you at Moreton-in-the-Marsh on the morning train. Be sure to be there!"

They nod.

* * * *

At Fitzjohns Avenue, all is arranged:

Peter is travelling down in Rupert, with the suitcases. Marg is following with Bill and Oswald on her motorbike-and-sidecar. Bill is to ride pillion, with Oswald taking pride of place in the sidecar.

It isn't quite what Oswald is used to but he's decided to treat it as a way to challenge his comfort zone.

Donning his Biggles helmet, sheepskin lined, leather flying jacket and goggles, Oswald climbs into the sidecar. Just for good measure, he's thrown a white silk scarf around his neck. Catching his image in the hall mirror on his way out, Oswald's secretly pleased with this latest fashion statement, there's no doubt about it, he cuts a fine figure of a bear!

Marg and Bill smile at his getup, as they walk to meet him. In complete contrast, they're kitted up in the latest in biking fashion. Black shiny visor helmets, black leathers and thick black leather biking boots.

Oswald's initial feeling, as they set out is alarm, as they speed down the motorway, overtaking speeding cars, large trucks and fast coaches. The countryside seems a blur, and he's constantly on the lookout for flashing blue lights.

Outside Oxford, Marg slows down as she negotiates the A44. The surrounding countryside is now clearly visible. Its lushness and fragrance enraptures him. The air seems cleaner, and - all about him - brighter and friendlier. He enjoys the stone walls, hedges, and picturesque villages; Woodstock, with its large palace, Chipping Norton, Bourton-on-the-Hill. What a contrast from city life with its dirt, grime, noise and pollution. The Heath is jolly nice with its lakes and ponds but not a patch on this. He watches a buzzard hover at the roadside; fixing its prey, and swooping for the kill. Life and death, they are part of the same - each a natural part of existence.

Without warning, a white van pulls out in front of them from a small side-road.

The sudden application of the brakes comes as a rude awakening, rocketing Oswald out of his reveries as he's propelled forward; the motorbike juddering to a halt.

"Fucking Idiot!!" Marg shouts.

With his chest pressing hard against his seatbelt, Oswald breaks wind.

Bill turns his helmet to face Oswald and peers at him, "Blimey, Oz! You farted!" he protests in a pained muffled voice, "That's a real beak-rumpler!"

Oswald, looking flustered, apologises, "I'm sorry, but I was startled."

"Well, just let me know when you're going to let another one of those go and I'll get off and walk," comes back the muffled reply.

"Wally Van Drivers! If you ask me, they've got their brains up their arses, if they've got brains!!" Checking the coast is clear, she overtakes the white-van driver, giving him the finger, as she passes.

Oswald, whose heart is all of a flutter, attempts to calm himself, by chanting a mantra.

Blaggit turns to his partner, "What's ruffled her feathers?"

Bodgit, having pulled out of the side-road without checking for oncoming traffic, turns to meet his partner's gaze, as he does so, he runs over a rabbit, squashing it flat, "Women Drivers! Fink they own the roads! A dose of the PMT if you asks me, ignore the tart!"

Blaggit, picking his nose, wonders what PMT is.

Feeling calmer, Oswald takes in some deep breaths and looks about him. 'Verdant,' he thinks to himself, 'there's no other word for it.'

Ever since the Oxford by-pass, Bill's been harbouring a strange feeling inside. He has butterflies in his stomach and is beginning to feel slightly on edge and nervous, though this has nothing to do with the near accident or Marg's handling of the bike. No, it's something less tangible. He can only describe it as a haunting feeling, a sense of impending doom, as if he's being watched, stalked! He shudders as a chill runs down his spine. 'Why do I feel so uncomfortable? What's my gut telling me?'

Once again, his morbid fear of death is resurfacing. 'I'm getting jittery in my old age,' he thinks. 'Come on, shake yourself out of it!'

Looking over at Oswald he smiles. Oz looks so cuddly and quaint snuggled up in the side-car, his scarf blowing behind him; a bit like a world war one fighter pilot in his cockpit-minus-the-wings. Bill chuckles to himself. He is really enjoying being in the company of his new friend. Oswald has an old world charm and innocence that is rare in these modern times.

Oswald waves and smiles at his friend, lost in his own thoughts.

As they travel towards their destination, faint stirrings are rattling around Bill's head, as distant memories tug at his consciousness. Bill wonders what's waiting for them at the mysterious circle of stones.

Some Memories, Dreams and Reflections

* * * *

Hannah leaves a message on the old analyst's machine cancelling her Tuesday appointment, "Hi! It's Hannah. Sorry for the last minute notice but I've been invited down to the country for a few days to stay with friends so I'll be unable to make Tuesday's session." There's a voice singing in the background, Hannah laughs, "Pipe down in there, I'm on the phone. Ooops! I'm still online…"

The line goes dead. The old analyst can't be sure but he thinks there's the sound of a young man singing and splashing water, in the background, in what sounds like the bathroom. It's nice to hear Hannah sounding happy and chirpy again, the country air will do her good.

Oswald's left a hand-delivered letter written in black ink on good quality headed note paper. It reads: 'Sorry for the short notice. I'm away for a week! Hope you don't mind? I look forward to our next session, on my return. Oswald Theodore Threadbare.'

Reading it, the analyst smiles. With this unexpected space he can visit his old friend, Helena. Perhaps she might be able to shed some light on his recurring dreams? It will be good to take coffee and catch up on what's going on with her, too. Nowadays, they only seem to meet at conferences and the occasional AJA meetings they attend. He reflects, 'it's an odd way to live one's life,' as he descends the stairs to meet his third analysand of the day, it's 9.30a.m.

* * * *

Marg's the first to arrive at the cottage. A postal strike has meant that the keys could not be sent through the post. Striding up the cottage path, she reads the note, written on the back of an envelope, pinned to the front door. 'Dear Peter and Marg, Please come up to the farmhouse for your keys, directions in envelope. Look forward to meeting you both. Best wishes, Adam Pyke.'

Oswald reads the newly painted name-plate on the wooden gate; 'Crumpleberry Cottage' "How quaint!" he says, to no-one in particular.

Climbing down from the bike, Bill stretches his legs, taking in the lay of the land.

The cottage is Cotswold stone with a thatched roof. It stands in a large well tended walled-garden, with its own vegetable patch. At the rear of the garden, there's a small mixed orchard. Bill looks at Oswald and gives the thumbs up, "Kind of dinky ain't it?"

Nodding in agreement, Oswald's keen eyesight, registers a cluster of large standing stones at the far end of the top field, at the side of the cottage, "Look over there!" he points in the direction of the stones, "If I'm not mistaken, those are standing stones."

"Geez, Oz! You must have the eyes of a hawk! If you hadn't pointed them out, they'd have remained a blur to me." Bill's sense of unease is returning. Something at the back of his mind is hammering, trying to get out. If only he can remember, then maybe he won't feel so cagey.

Walking back towards the bike, Marg takes off her helmet and shakes out her hair. It glistens in the afternoon sun. She shows the note to her companions, "You two staying here, or coming along for the ride?"

To Oswald's surprise, Bill suggest they accompany Marg.

Marg senses Bill's unease, "You okay, Bill?"

"I think it might be a good idea if we all kept together for the time being, don't you?"

"Sure!" Marg looks to Oswald who shrugs and climbs into the side-car.

Marg rides the three miles to the farmhouse pulling up in the yard.

Stepping out to greet them, Mr Pyke shakes them warmly by the hand, "I hope you had a good journey down? If you'd like to step into the kitchen I've got the kettle on the boil, perhaps I can offer you a cup of tea?"

"It's kind of you to offer, Mr Pyke but we need to get back to the cottage for Pete. He'll need help with the cases."

Mr Pyke offers them the keys, "Of course! He'll probably be wondering what's happened to you? I'm sorry about the hassle with the keys."

"It's not your fault, Mr Pyke!" she gives him a reassuring smile.

"These things happen. Well! We'd best get on."

As Marg rides off, Mr Pyke calls out to her and her companions, "If there's anything you need, don't hesitate to call, anything at all." He waves.

Mrs Eelbake's cycling back from her Great Aunt Tilley's ("I'm ninety-seven, you know!") Passing Mr Pyke's farmyard on her way home. Always keen to know what's going on locally, she takes in the scene, stopping by the roadside, she watches farmer Pyke with the young woman and her two strange companions.

Spotting her, Mr Pyke groans inwardly and forces a smile. He gives her a wave. Mrs Eelbake offers a polite smile and mounting her push-bike, peddles as fast as her feet will go, in the direction of 'Bideawee', the residence of her friend and mentor, Miss Gossip.

* * * *

They are exploring the cottage when Peter arrives. Marg runs out to greet him, giving him a large hug and passionate kiss on the lips, "It's a great place we've rented, I love it! What kept you so long, I've missed you! Wait till you see our bedroom, its real cosy."

Peter laughs and points to the groceries and luggage, "I've missed you too, but how about some help with all this?"

Marg kisses him fully on the lips pressing her eager body against his. She gives a contented sigh, "Okay, I guess I'll have to save it for later."

Peter shakes his head with pleasure and picking up two suitcases makes his way to the door, "You're on a definite promise," he smiles.

"I'm counting on it," Marg picks up a box of groceries and follows him in.

All unpacked and rooms allocated, with very little coaxing, the two lovers set off to find the local Inn, while Oswald and Bill stay behind, to prepare a slap-up meal.

Weary from their journeys, checking out the local pub and chatting with the locals seems the ideal way to spend some time before dinner.

Oswald and Bill wave them off. Glancing at each other, they give an affectionate sigh at the sight of their young friends blossoming love. Sauntering up the garden path, arms linked, they share their impressions of the cottage and of their journey down.

The cottage has a charm all of its own. Its bright shiny windows give the place a welcoming sort of smile. Inside, it's spotless, with all the modern conveniences, fresh and cosy. The kitchen's large and airy. On the pine-scrubbed table stands a large blue vase full of freshly picked wild flowers. Oswald puts on his navy-blue, white-striped apron, while Bill browses through some recipe books. Their holiday has begun.

* * * *

The meal and evening are a great success.

That night, all within Crumpleberry, are blessed with the deep peaceful sleep of the innocent.

In the fields outside ghostly coloured lights circle the stones.

* * * *

Always an early riser, Marg sets about opening the curtains, letting in the new day. Brilliant sunlight fills the rooms.

Bill, groggy with sleep, looks out from under his duvet and watches Marg draw his curtains and open his bedroom window, "Sling yer hook, will yer!"

Marg just laughs, placing a glass of his favourite fruit juice on his bedside cabinet, "Morning Bill!"

It's always amazed Bill how Marg could be so cheerful at such an early hour, it's scary. Catching the time on his wristwatch, he groans and buries himself under his bedcovers. "Go away!" he muffles.

Oswald is much more appreciative, thanking her for his glass of hot water. He watches the beams of light filter through the window, the fine dust dancing on its shafts. As Marg opens his window, Oswald breathes in deeply, filling his lungs with fresh air. Marg smiles, seeing him, propped up against his fluffed-up white pillows, dressed in his pale blue striped pyjamas. She always sleeps in the buff and wonders how anybody can get a good night's kip with clothes on? Still, the English are a funny lot.

Oswald reaches for his glass and sips his hot water.

"Are you sure you wouldn't like something stronger?"

Oswald smiles, "No thank you Marg, this will do me nicely."

Peter is the same. First thing in the morning and the last thing at night, he sips a glass of hot water. As they are getting used to each other, she asks him about the hot water. He tells her that his nanny had always insisted, " 'It will keep you regular and give you a clear complexion,' she told me."

Marg has to admit; he does have lovely skin and a fine complexion.

"Why are the Brits so obsessed with their bowel movements?" she'd once asked Bill.

After some consideration Bill had responded, "They're kind of cut-off from their emotions, self-absorbed and up their own arses, half he time, if you ask me Marg. Now, if you'll excuse me, I'm going for a dump."

"Fancy coming for a jog, Oz?" Marg enquires hopefully.

Oswald looks at his bulging tummy, "Yes!" he says, surprising himself, "Why not!"

"You will?" somewhat taken aback Marg is delighted.

Marg talks Oswald through some warm-up exercises, before the actual jog. Stretching, to try and touch his toes, Oswald wonders if he's been wise, volunteering his company for such an energetic venture, so early in the morning. He's definitely out of condition and needs to drop a few pounds - well, perhaps a stone or two. He wonders if jogging is the best way. Perhaps he ought to take up Yoga or Tai-Chi, when he gets back - if he gets back! He's exhausted already and they've only just finished what Marg's described as 'a few gentle warm-up exercises.' What's it going to be like when they start running?"

Marg promises that she'll keep the pace steady. She's certainly in good shape. Oswald thinks she looks quite fetching in her jogging gear.

* * * *

That afternoon:

Mrs Eelbake and Miss Gossip compare notes as they sit in the garden of 'Bideawee,' sipping Lapsong Souchong from Miss Gossip's finest bone china, and nibbling scones.

"A black leather, tight fitting top, and tight leather pants with a zip that pulls all the way down the front! And her, a young lady too! Astride a motorbike! Big. Black. And Throbbing, it was. Covered in chrome!"

Miss Gossip, heart all of a flutter, interrupts, "Well! You should have seen what I saw this morning! I tell you! No word of a lie! An affront to the fairer sex, I say! A baggy yellow vest, with no support, and pink baggy shorts. You could see her wotsits when she bent down!"

Mrs Eelbake drops her scone, "Never! Not her wotsits? You don't say!"

Miss Gossip watches the scone roll down the lawn and into the flowerbed, "I'm telling you, Mrs Eelbake, that's not all! They are tanned! Sun-tanned! Would you believe it?"

"Sun-tanned?"

Miss Gossip gives a solemn nod.

"Well! I'll go to the foot of our stairs! Whatever next?" Mrs Eelbake stirs her tea vigorously

* * * *

Marg helps Oswald, as he hobbles up the garden path, after their jog. Red-faced and short of breath, he looks exhausted.

Peter's looking out for them. With Bill's help he's prepared a delicious breakfast of yogurt, fresh fruit, home-baked bread, fresh farm butter, strawberry conserve, almond croissants, piping hot fresh ground coffee and freshly squeezed orange juice.

While Marg finishes her morning workout; Oswald, aching in places he never knew he had, makes his way upstairs to take a long soak in the tub.

* * * *

Breakfast's enjoyed by all:

Oswald, is feeling rather sleepy, from all the exercise and too many croissants. He excuses himself from the table intending to take a short nap outside, on a blanket, on the garden lawn. "Hopefully the sun will ease one or two of my aches," he informs them.

Marg and Peter plan to explore the surrounding countryside and its little villages. They'll be out for the best part of the day.

Insisting, they leave clearing the breakfast things away to him, Bill sends them on their way, "Oz and I are going to do some mooching around ourselves later," he informs them, as he waves them off.

Handing his car-keys over to Marg, Peter and Marg set off in Rupert. Marg takes the wheel. They seem happy in each others company on this sun-kissed day.

Putting up a shade, Bill places it over his friend, protecting him from the worst effects of the sun and, returning to the kitchen, sets about doing the dishes.

* * * *

In his dream, Oswald is airborne, flying down a deep winding canyon, carved through a great mountain range. Dark, ancient rocks tower skywards, their peaks hidden by clouds. Slowly, carefully, Oswald makes his way along the winding curves, scanning the terrain above and below; moving onward, deeper into the folds of grey, rocky mass. All about him he can see nothing but steep grey stone, a terrain broken only by texture; no life.

He passes through jagged struts with their razor-sharp edges; huge mountains of shale and slate, sheer grained walls of greyness. Everything seems still, dull, dormant.

From time to time, a cold chill comes upon him, as if a dark cloud has passed over the sun, barring its warmth. Even the air hangs in silence.

Moving onwards, the canyon opens out into a large circle surrounded by huge, shiny boulders. In the centre he can just make out what looks like the warm glow of a camp fire. Cautiously, Oswald makes his descent towards the flickering lights. As he draws closer, he becomes aware of another's presence. Seated beside the fire is the solitary figure of the old Indian. On his approach the old man neither looks up nor stirs. His gaze is fixed intently on the heart of the blaze.

Oswald seats himself opposite the old man. Feeling a great hunger and thirst come upon him, he helps himself to food and drink. Life-affirming, the nourishment fills his body with an energy and vitality that enhances his strength, sharpening his senses.

For the first time, aware of the subtle energies flowing about him, Oswald waits for the old man, fixing his eyes upon his every move. Patterns of light dance upon the old man's deep-lined face. Oswald is aware of a great wisdom behind this impassive mask.

The place is alive with energy. Looking up from the fire, the old Indian looks deep into Oswald's eyes; the windows of his soul. What he sees is an inner flame, pure and bright. Smiling, the old man welcomes his friend, "Welcome to the place of No-thing. The All That Is. That of which all comes and in which all is contained."

"We meet again, Old Teacher. How can this be? Surely I am

dreaming?"

"Where are you seated?" the old man asks.

"Why! In the centre of this great circle." Looking about him Oswald waves his paw.

"You are seated in the centre of your own circle of awareness; the awakening of your unconscious."

"Why am I here?"

"The Great Mother has need of you and your friends."

"Is she in peril?"

"There are forces abroad, that would do her and her children harm."

"Then tell me, how can we help?"

"Find the place of perfect balance and harmony."

"Where shall we find this place you speak of?"

"In the silence, where the power of knowing is and where the answer to your needs, and the harmony you seek, lie hidden."

"Does this place have a name?"

The old Indian smiles, as the scene begins to fade, leaving Oswald alone, in a dark tunnel. He calls out again, "Old man! Old man! By what name shall we know this place?"

Carried on the distant breeze, comes the sigh, "Within."

* * * *

Having finished the dishes and cleared away the breakfast things, Bill looks out of the window to check on his friend. Oswald's lying on the lawn, still asleep, waving his paw in the air, his body rocking from side to side.

Bill looks out upon the scene. A large blue butterfly flutters around the sleeping bear, as if, inspecting the sleeping form. Satisfied with its reconnaissance, the butterfly lands on Oswald's nose. Quivering and twitching, Oswald's nose erupts into a sneeze. Sensing the convulsions, the large blue butterfly removes its presence from the bear's rhinal area, observing the explosion with disdain.

Oswald opens his eyes but the butterfly has flown.

Knocking on the kitchen window, Bill holds up the teapot.

Arising from his slumbers, Oswald brushes himself down and walks towards the kitchen. Over a hot cup of tea, Oswald recounts his dream.

* * * *

Summoning his P.A., Lord Itsmyne instructs:

"Sharpe! You are to spend the weekend in the Cotswolds. I want you to observe the stones. I'll expect your report first thing Monday morning!"

Receiving his instructions in silence, Grabbitall-Sharpe sets about his task with a heavy heart. He had been hoping to spend the weekend on his boat with Samantha. It'll just have to be a pleasure postponed. The chore must come first.

Within four hours, he's checking into the 'Dog and Duck', a discreet Inn full of old world charm and weekend couples signed in under the name of 'Smith.'

* * * *

Mrs Steelman replaces the receiver on its cradle, adrenalin coursing through her veins. What did they mean? They'd send somebody around later! Her neighbour had been burgled! How did she know? Why, their front curtains had moved and no, they didn't have a pet! Sure! SURE!!! Of course she was sure! If they didn't come around right away, she'd phone her M.P. And yes, she did have a direct line! Perhaps they'd like to explain their reticence to her!

Twenty minutes later, a rather plump constable dismounts his bicycle, trudges up the path, peers through the windows and tries the door.

Mrs Steelman waits by his cycle.

Within five minutes of entering, he's radioed for a police car. The house has been burgled. It looks like a professional job. P.C. Dobbs takes out his notebook, while Mrs Steelman dictates.

It is 7 a.m., Sunday morning, when the men-in-blue knock on the door of Crumpleberry Cottage.

Peter steps into his jeans and goes down to answer. It's going to be another fine sunny day.

Constables, Black and White greet him as he opens the door; it's the end of their shift.

Peter looks somewhat startled, "Is something wrong constables?"

P.C. Black the older of the two, steps forward, "Doctor Peter

Lawrence?"

"Yes."

"May we come in, sir?"

Standing aside; Peter let's them in, "Of course, what's this all about?" he leads them into the kitchen.

P.C. White shows him a report chart, with his address on, "Are you the owner of this property in London?"

"Yes I am. What's happened?"

It was P.C. Black's turn, "We're sorry to inform you, but you've been burgled."

Peter runs his hand through his hair, "Shit! When did this happen?"

P.C. White hands him a card with a telephone number on it, "If you telephone this number, they'll give you all the details sir."

Thanking them, Peter shows them out.

Sleepily, Marg climbs down the stairs; she has nothing on, "What's going on? Who were those two guys?"

Peter gives her a pained smile, taking in her beauty, "They were the police, come to tell me that our London place has been burgled. It looks like I'll have to return to Hampstead to check it out, sorry!"

Marg rains down a torrent of Aussie expletives upon the heads of the perpetrators, holding Peter close to her. It dawns on Peter that he's done something that he thought he'd never do again, fallen in love.

Showered and dressed, they break the news to Bill and Oswald. Peter suggests they remain at the cottage while he travels back to London to check it out. Marg is having none of it, Oz and Bill should stay but she's going back with him. They'll return as soon as things are sorted.

With sad heart's Bill and Oswald wave the two lovers off, later that morning.

"Apologise to Hannah for us!" Peter shouts, as Marg clunks Rupert's gears.

"We will." Bill assures them.

Oswald winces at Marg's rough handling of Rupert's gears. He turns to Bill, "I think mine's fallen in love with yours."

"I think mines fallen in love with yours too."

They smile.

* * * *

Thanks to the energetic company of Mandy, (wayward younger daughter of the late beloved local squire), Henry's stay at the 'Dog and Duck' has been rather enjoyable.

She picked him up in the lounge just after he'd checked in, on Friday evening. Satiated, glowing from top to toe, pleasantly exhausted, she'd put him down, late Sunday morning in time for brunch in their room:

Henry's loin's stirs, as she saunters out of the bathroom dressed in a skimpy white cotton thong. Stretching her lithe, full-breasted body, she raises her arms above her head. Her sexual energy is electric, as she revels in the power she holds over men. Turning her back, she wriggles her firm perfectly formed bottom at him. Cupping her pendulous breasts, she begins to caress herself. Henry pleads for her to come back to bed, but Mandy just giggles and shakes her head. Finding her designer jeans, she steps into them.

"If you won't come back to bed, how about taking a stroll, with me, to the standing stones?"

"I'd love to darling, you know that, but…"

"You have to pick your boyfriend up from the station, I know." Henry seems resigned. He watches her as she slowly pulls her tight fitting T-shirt over her ample breasts. "He's a lucky man!"

Mandy shakes her curly mop of raven black hair. Her erect nipples push at the straining T-shirt, "Isn't he just, darling," her voice is low and sultry. Picking up her jacket she casually slings it over her shoulder. "Think of me, while you're on your nice walk, slaving over a hard, firm, body." Blowing him a kiss, she gives him a wicked smile, closes the door behind her and leaves his life, as casually as she'd entered it.

Henry Grabbitall-Sharpe realises that he's met his match in Mandy. Sighing, he climbs out of bed and makes his way towards the shower. This afternoon he has work to do.

Parking his car by the lay-by, Henry opens the gate, and makes his way across the field towards the five stones, locally known as the Whispering Knights.

Once again, it's turned out to be a hot sunny day. The afternoon sun feels oppressive, the air is still, and for the first time, Henry notices the silence. There's no sound of life at all.

His mind wanders back to Mandy. He wonders what she's doing now, although he has a good idea. Her energy and insatiable appetite both thrill and sadden him. In many ways they are alike, both have a need to fill their lives with more, mistakenly equating sensations for life, orgasms for love. He wonders if she ever feels empty inside, despite her sensations- packed- life.

He knows he does, for, no matter how much wealth and power he accrues, there's still a nagging pain; a hunger, that bores away at him, constantly urging him forward, in pursuit of more power, more wealth. It's like trying to fill a bottomless pit.

At times, these feelings overwhelm him, intoxicating him, so that he feels he no longer knows himself or the direction in which he is heading. All he can be sure of, at these times, is that he wants more, needs more, must have more! Greed is his drug and want his addiction.

Itsmyne has been a good teacher.

Henry stops and listens. Nothing! No birds, no insects, no animals, not even the sound of a car. This place has become isolated, cut-off, desolate. As he approaches the stones, he becomes aware of the sense of menace pervading the place. His body shivers.

Henry Grabbitall-Sharpe feels distinctly uncomfortable and a little frightened. Slowly, his senses are invaded with a creeping, irrational sense of fear, coupled with hatred.

Glancing away from the Whispering Knights, he sees the welcoming sight of the ancient circle of standing stones. Instinctively, he moves towards them, even paced at first; fearful of looking back, for to look back would be to see something that he really does not want to see. He quickens his pace, aware of the concentrated malice behind him, willing him to look back.

As the sun bears down from a cloudless sky, Henry Grabbitall-Sharpe feels the fingers of an icy chill, crawl upon his body, reaching out to grasp at the warmth of his heart. Panicking, he begins to run towards the safety of the stone circle, demonic laughter filling his ears.

Unable to maintain any semblance of calm, he races through the tall grass, his heart pounding in his chest, fear gripping him. He is being chased! He has an urge to see his pursuers. Looking back over his shoulder, the recognition startles him. It is the shame and ugliness of his greed seeking him out, pressing down upon him. Its foul stench invades his nostrils.

He cries out in pain, panic and fear spurring him on. He must get to the circle! The agony of his past stalks him, howling with demonic glee, as it gains. Henry's heart pounds in his chest, one last push, that's all that's needed.

This cannot be all that he is? No! He is much, much more! Terrified of the ugly self, pursuing him, Henry vows to change.

Surging forward he bounds over the metal fence, safe in the circle of stones: CALM.

Once more he can hear the songs of the birds, the busy sounds of insects. Terrified and shaken, Henry slumps in the circle, pressing his body to the earth. Breathless, he chokes back his fear. The emptiness that has lain hidden, deep, deep inside him floods his body. Corrupt and sordid, his past has met up with him, and he's filled with shame.

Safe within the circle now, he weeps like a child, contrite; in need. The heat of the sun warms his wracked body, thawing the ice from his heart. Lying on the simple ground his emptiness is replaced with hope, the feel of the earth soothes his troubled mind.

* * * *

Jackie Pringle is helping the police with their enquiries.

She has been a bad girl! She's thrown a stale porkpie at the Prime Minister. He was reading a statement to the press outside his official holiday residence, Chequers:

"No! I don't think there is any imminent danger from the comet. Yes! The situation is being closely monitored."

It was as he was turning to the cameras to give one of his disarming smiles that the projectile struck him, smack in the eye. As he fell, he clutched at the offending object, gripping it tightly in his right hand. It had a message attached to it.

Questioned by the press, Jackie Pringle said she was protesting at being made homeless. She'd lived at Sunnyside Psychiatric Hospital for twenty years but the government insisted that she should be released back into the care of the community, and now she lived on the streets.

"It isn't fair! Nobody asked me what I wanted! Nergal's told me that the world is going to end next week so, I wanted to get my own back before it does. We're all DOOMED you know! WE ARE!!!"

Smiling at the cameras she was whisked away by the police.

* * * *

The swelling is going down. The P.M's bruised, but not yet beaten:

Taking the offending object from his pocket he reads the attached message: "You're DOOMED!!" it reads. He forces a weak smile and puts the porkpie on the table, beside him in the Cabinet Room. The Deputy Prime Minister eyes the porkpie with undisguised interest.

It's been a busy day. He looks at his assembled ministers in the cabinet office. "Would I buy a second-hand car from any of these toadies?" He thinks not!

* * * *

Around the planet, high-level conferences are taking place in other government offices, mostly in secret. Planet Earth is under threat! The comet is on a direct collision course. N.A.S.A. has told the President that all anyone can do is cross their fingers, hope for the best, and wait.

Mr President crosses his fingers.

* * * *

As the Prime Minister calls the meeting to order, the Cabinet Secretary commiserates on his 'shiner'. His ministers smirk. He looks to his Press Officer, who gives them one of his withering looks. Rubbing his cheek, The Chancellor of the Exchequer, gives him the finger.

Uncomfortable, the others squirm in their seats.

"Okay you guys, you've all been briefed on the situation." As he glances around at the assembled they all nod. "Are there any suggestions?"

The Minister for Culture raises her hand. With a look of devotion in her eyes, she suggests, "Might we not blame it on the incompetence of the last Government?"

The P.M. wonders if a hurtling fiery comet, on a collision course towards Earth isn't such a bad thing, after all.

* * * *

It is Monday morning:

Lord Itsmyne studies Henry's report. It was on his desk, waiting for him as he arrived, first thing. Looking up from it he smiles. There's something of the night about him. A dark cloud passes behind his eyes.

* * * *

Hannah spots her two companions, as soon as she steps down

from the train:

Oswald's World War One, fighter pilot outfit and Bill's black leather biker gear ensures that they stand out in a crowd. She wonders if they're hiding something from her about the exact nature of their relationship…

The weather is hot, very hot! On the news, it's been reported that freak atmospheric conditions are causing havoc with the weather patterns around the world and might possibly affect climatic condition throughout the whole of the U.K.

Hannah loves the sun. It makes her feel horny. Her last two days have been what can only be described as steamy. Her young beau certainly has lived up to his pony-tail and proved to be a bit of a wild stallion. She'd certainly enjoyed breaking him in!

And yet, now, it's she who feels broken, broken inside. She's come down from her 'high', as she knew she would, and feels empty inside. She's hoping that Bill and Oswald might be able to lift her spirits. Their bizarre outfits make her grin from ear to ear; already their charm is working on her.

Oswald's the first to step forward to greet her, taking her rucksack from her shoulder.

Hannah smiles, "Always the gentleman, Oswald."

Nodding gracefully, Oswald hands the rucksack to Bill.

Bill gives him a sidelong glance, "Geeze, thanks Oz!"

Oswald smiles beneficently. Hooking his arm under Hannah's, he walks her out of the train station, Bill struggling behind.

Hannah laughs, when she sees the motorbike and side-car. She beseeches them imploringly, her hands pressed together in supplication, "Oh, please, please, please… let me ride the bike back to the cottage?"

Her two companions look at each other.

"But you don't know the directions!" Oswald says.

It's now Bill's turn to be the gentleman, "No matter, Oz, I can give her directions as we go."

Hannah can't contain her joy and jumping up and down, claps her hands, "Oh, goody!"

Her two companions shrug and smile. Hannah has a knack of making them feel special. Her enthusiasm's infectious. Anyway, what harm can it do?

With Hannah at the controls, the return journey back to Crumpleberry Cottage, even with Bill giving directions, knocks two thirds off the running time that it took to get to the station. Exhilarated; Hannah pulls up outside the cottage to the sound of screeching brakes, the motorbike and side-car skidding to a halt!

Clambering down from the pillion, Bill falls to the ground, kissing it repeatedly as if it's a long lost Italian cousin.

Oswald climbs out of the side-car with dignity. In a daze, mirroring disbelief, he makes his way crookedly - on two very wobbly legs - up the cottage path, attempting to take in deep breaths along the way.

Hannah, throwing off her helmet, gives a laugh, deep from

inside her belly; the adrenalin rush has made her come alive!

Mechanically, Oswald and Bill disrobe their bikers gear and set about making tea. Both have seen their lives passing before them on their return journeys. Oswald feels as if he's still left a part of himself back at the station car-park. Bill wonders what happens to duck-billed platypuses once they come out of shock. While Hannah feels pleasantly hungry.

* * * *

Stealthily, the weather changes. A fine mist creeps along the fields as the clear blue sky fills with clouds.

* * * *

Two cups of tea down the line:

Oswald and Bill are beginning to feel more settled in themselves, the palpitations have gone and the shock subsided.

Hannah listens with interest, as they tell her their news, "Have you visited the standing stones yet?" she asks.

Bill seems uneasy, "Actually, we've been waiting for you before we do that."

Hannah's touched by Bill's response, but then she notices the puzzled look Oswald's giving him.

It's Bill who first notices the change in the weather. Sensing that Hannah's picked up his unease around the stones, he wishes to deflect her and change the topic of conversation. Standing up, he moves towards the window to check the weather to see if it's too hot to take lunch in the garden. To his utter surprise, he finds the window covered with a thin white veil of translucent mist. He opens the door to check that it's not smoke from a bonfire. "Stone the crows!" He turns to his companions, "Come and check this out! The weather's changed! You're not going to believe this!"

Oswald peers out, "Good Heavens! It's misty! What do you make of this Hannah?"

Hannah steps out into the garden, closely followed by the others. She looks about her. The mist is everywhere. It feels warm and clammy - a bit like being in a sauna. It wasn't like this in her dreams; the weather had always been fine. She turns to Oswald and Bill, "Have either of you seen the weather reports or heard the news today?"

Looking at each other, they shrug, "No?" they reply.

Hannah casts her mind back to the early morning news briefing, "I think it's better if we go inside and talk."

Bill takes Oswald's arm and looks about uncomfortably, "Yeah, I reckon you might be right. I don't like the vibes I'm getting out here. If you ask me, something weird's going on around here. What do you say, Oz?"

Oswald looks about him, "Yes, one does feel strange in this setting, I must admit!"

In his minds-eye, a vision of the old American Indian appears and the aroma of sweet grass and sage permeate his nostrils. A chill runs down Oswald's spine and he knows what he has to do.

"Hannah's right, let's go in!"

Wishing to protect the cottage and it's occupants from the negative energies amassing outside, Oswald sets about countering the energy, by cleansing the cottage, in the manner the old American Indian taught him. Lighting a candle, he fetches his backpack from his room.

Hannah looks on, intrigued, as Oswald and Bill set about the purification ritual. The two of them place pots of sage and sweet-grass, strategically, in each room and light them. Then, producing three smudge sticks, Oswald lights them, and instructs his two friends as to their use. Room by room they purify the cottage. When they've finished, they smudge each other.

Fine-tuning himself to their energies, Oswald uses his rattle, a gift from the old Indian, to smooth out his companions auras; removing the barriers between perception of the material world and the realms of spiritual realities. Hidden memories tell him that this will create a bridge they'll need to accomplish the work that they have been brought here to do.

When he's finished, Oswald looks at his two friends and smiles, "It's done! Now it's safe to begin our quest. We can talk now."

Making themselves comfortable, Hannah recounts what she's heard on the early news. She also reports a conversation she's had with Carl, her weekend guest. A freelance reporter and blogger, he's told her that the Government are trying to hold back a big news story. The scent's out that there is a big cover-up going on, possibly global, that the world's governments want to keep the wraps on.

Famished, Bill suggests that they talk over lunch, "I don't know about you two, but my belly's beginning to feel that my throats been cut!"

Hannah, remembering her hunger agrees, "Sounds good to me." The three chattering companions set about preparing their lunch.

* * * *

Mrs Eelbake's cycling home when the mist descends. Now she's not even sure if she's going in the right direction. Feeling silly and annoyed with herself; everything seems different cloaked in this fine mist. Of course she's going in the right direction, whatever does she think she's playing at? How can one get lost in one's own home district? She's been taking this route for more years than she cares to remember! If only she could get her bearings though. She'll be telling herself next, that she's lost! Whatever would her dear departed Herbert say? She gives a forced chuckle. You know what he'd say, don't you?

"Moll doll," he'd say, "I think you've gone and got yourself a case of the jitters." She smiles at the thought of him but the bitterness of his loss encroaches.

Thirty years service he'd given to Itsmine Global. The best years of his life. He'd had to take early retirement from the chemical plant, due to ill health. When they retired they'd always planned to buy a cottage in the Cotswolds, in the village where they'd both grown up. However, things don't always work out as planned or hoped for. Within six months of retirement Moll's Herbert was dead. The young doctor reckoned that the lining of her Herbert's lungs had corroded away.

The doctor had tried to persuade Mrs Eelbake to take out an action against Itsmine Global for compensation, but she didn't, "It just doesn't seem right to bite the hand that's fed you," she'd argued. The doctor shrugged and dropped the matter.

Now Mrs Eelbake feels bitter at her loss. He'd been a good husband and her life seems empty without him. She misses him so much! Just the thought of him makes her tearful, "Pull yourself together!" she tells herself. "You'll cope! You always do, just keep peddling! This mist is just another of life's many trials."

She musters her strength and sharpens her resolve. She'll listen out for the sound of traffic. It had been a fine sunny day when she'd set out from her friend's, Miss Gossip's! She'd worn her new summer dress and light cardigan, now she's beginning to feel damp and clammy from the mist. "Great Aunt Tilly was right! The weather has never been right since they sent people into space, no it hasn't!"

In the distance, she can see a dark red glowing light. She wonders where she is. Her legs feel as if she's been peddling uphill for the last ten minutes, at least. She's beginning to feel tired and a little frightened; surely she'll see a familiar landmark, or a sign that will tell her where she is soon? The hill seems to be levelling out; she must be close to Mr Pyke's place and her little cottage. There it is the lay-by! She must be close to the ancient stone site.

Over the way, is the field where the Whispering Knights stand, she'll soon be home! Peering through the mist, she looks in their direction.

'What's that red glow coming from the field?'

Mrs Eelbake stops peddling and puts her foot to the ground, steadying her bicycle.

The glow has the hue of thick red blood and seems to be getting stronger. Now, it's easier to make out. It's coming from the centre of the five stones. Their outlines are clearly visible through the rolling mist. She gasps, her heart leaping into her mouth, the five stones are alive and moving towards her, they're growing bigger and bigger! Their energy is seeking her out, reaching out to touch her. Their intensity sends a cold chill down her spine. She can feel the coldness in their hearts and it frightens her. Hate, pure hate, oozes from them.

Mrs Eelbake feels stifled. A hidden fear, deep from somewhere inside her, fills her whole being with terror and dread. Unable to control her shaking, she turns her bike around and peddles with all of her strength. She feels that she has to get away from this place, these stones, or whatever they have become! She must escape them, or else…!

Peddling with all her might, adrenalin fuelling her every move, she races back down the hill from whence she has come. They will not have her! They shall not make her as their own! She will change! Let go of all her bitterness! Looking back over her shoulder, she can see their faint glow in the distance. They are mocking her! Laughing at her pain! Distance! She must put distance between her and them. Capture is not an option! Terrified, a loud bursting wail issues from her mouth, as tears roll down her ashen face. Seeking solace, she recites the twenty-third psalm, "The Lord's my shepherd, I shall not want…" as she speeds away from the menace behind her, towards the cottage lights in the distance.

Now desperate, what she seeks most is safety and refuge!

* * * *

After a very pleasant lunch of fresh pasta, with Bill's home-made pesto, mixed salad, with Oswald's special Italian dressing, oven baked ciabatto, fresh olives and parmesan; followed by fresh raspberries, crème fraiche and pots of ground coffee; the company of three sit round the kitchen table and set about trying to make sense of their collected knowledge.

It's Hannah who leads the conversation:

"We've been brought here for a reason; I think we're all agreed on this?"

Bill and Oswald nod their agreement.

Hannah continues, "I reckon that whatever we're supposed to be doing has to be in some way connected to this location and the standing stones."

Oswald interjects, "I think you'll find that they are central to it! In my dream the old Indian told me Mother Earth had need of us. I think something bad is about to happen."

"Something local, national or global, Oz?" Bill enquires.

"Carl alluded to something big!" Hannah chips in.

"Really big?" Bill says.

Hannah nods.

"Geez!" Bill hisses through his beak, "We're talking global, aren't we?"

"We are!" Oswald confirms. "And, not disaster, more…"

"Catastrophe?" Hannah offers, her voice quiet and thoughtful.

Oswald gives a shrug.

"It makes sense; the media is full of 'The End of the World' stories." Bill says, "Although, up till now I put them down to millennium fever. Now, I'm not so sure!" Bill looks at his two companions. Hannah's deep in thought, worrying about Willow. Frowning, she bites her bottom lip.

"There's been a lot of talk about comets, of late." Oswald says.

Lifting her head, Hannah looks at them, "You don't think it's connected, do you?"

Bill looks concerned and slightly troubled, recalling Marg's early dreams, "It might sound crazy, but right now, I don't think we can rule anything out."

"No matter how wild it seems?" asks Oswald.

"Right!" says Bill, nodding in Oswald's direction.

"You'll probably think me nuts, but I'm kind of excited and scared, all at the same time." Hannah owns.

Oswald focuses his two friends, "The question is; what are we going to do? We need to go and investigate the standing stones!"

The others assent.

Oswald picks up Bill's reticence, "You seem in two minds Bill?"

"To tell you the truth Oz, I am! It's just a feeling, but my gut's telling me to leave them well alone. It sounds irrational, but there's something lurking out there that I really don't want to meet."

"Like a monster or something?" Hannah's wide-eyed.

"To be honest, I don't know what it is! I only know that I'm in no great hurry to meet it."

"How fascinating," Hannah's intrigued.

"I guess that's one way of looking at it, gal!" Bill's eyes meet Hannah's. He gives her a worried smile.

Sensing a drop in energy levels, Oswald tries to rally their spirits, "So, what's our plan of campaign?"

"I guess we pay the stones a visit?" Bill says.

A sudden thumping on the door makes all three jump.

As one, they get up from the table and make their way to the door, to see what all the commotion is about. Opening it, Bill stands back, as Mrs Eelbake bursts in on them; damp, sobbing and shaking with fear. Clinging to Oswald, she stares back over her shoulder - her body rigid - a look of terror on her face. "Please! Close the door! Lock it! Don't let them get me!" she begs.

"There, there, everything's going to be okay, you're safe here! Come away from the door and let me take you into the kitchen. What you need is a nice hot cup of tea!" Oswald leads her into the kitchen. Bill fills the kettle and puts it on the Aga to boil.

Curious at this sudden visitation, Hannah peers out into the mist. Apart from the distressed woman's bicycle, there's nothing much out there to be seen. Shrugging, she closes the door firmly behind her. A sudden chill catches her body. Shaking off a shudder, she follows the others into the kitchen, "Someone must be standing on my grave," she says to herself.

It's sometime before they can get the woman to give her name. Bill offers her a mug of strong, hot, sweet tea.

Cradling the mug in her hands, she draws comfort and strength from its heat. Sipping it, she begins to settle and become calmer. Looking about her, she takes in her surroundings, studying the faces of those around her.

After finishing her tea, Hannah takes her up to her room, to change out of her damp clothes and into some of Hannah's dry warm clothes.

Bill and Oswald wait for them in the kitchen.

Hannah's lends Mrs Eelbake a pair of faded blue jeans, a cornflower blue T-shirt and a pink, hand-knitted top. Using her blow-dryer, she helps to dry the old woman's damp, dishevelled hair.

Hannah's clothes make the old woman look ten years younger. Less agitated, a little lightness flows back into her soul. Feeling calmer, she sits around the cosy kitchen table with the three kind strangers. Mrs Eelbake feels the need to share her tale.

Explaining how it all happened, she tells them about the light.

"You saw a light?" Oswald queries.

"Yes! Blood red it was - menacing! Gets right inside you, churns you up, it's awful!" Looking at the gathered, she continues her tale. "It was in the field, by the five stones. I couldn't help it! Stopping my bike, I got off to have a closer look. The light seemed to want me to come closer. It was drawing me towards it! Powerful it was, awful hard. I felt as if I was being pulled towards it. They were calling to me!"

"The five stones?" Bill asks.

"Yes, the Whispering Knights!"

The assembled four look at each other.

"What happened next?" Hannah asks, eyes as big as saucers.

Mrs Eelbake begins to sob. "You'll think me mad! A foolish old woman, who ought to know better!"

Oswald offers her a tissue, "Here, dry your eyes. Nobody's going to think anything of the sort, please, do continue," his voice is kind and reassuring.

Bill and Hannah's eyes meet fleetingly, there's amazement in them. Each take a hand and give it a reassuring squeeze.

Mastering her fear, Mrs Eelbake lets out a jagged sigh, "The light seemed to glow and flicker."

"You mean pulsate?" Hannah asked.

"Yes! That's it, pulsate. It was in the midst of the Knights, sending out a sort of signal. I rubbed my eyes. I thought I was losing my wits… but, it's the truth, I tell you! Them stones was growing, getting bigger and, I swear they were moving!"

"Moving?" queries Oswald.

"They were weaving in and out of one another," she stops to think. "Yes! It was like they were dancing…"

"Dancing?" Hannah's bemused.

Mrs Eelbake looks at Hannah, wide-eyed and fearful, "Do you think I'm going mad?"

Bill gives her hand another squeeze and shakes his head.

Comforted and reassured she continues, "I knew I wasn't daft; but I saw what I saw! The knights, I mean the stones… oh; I don't know what I mean… The stones were alive, they were moving!"

"Alive as in 'alive'?" asks Oswald.

"Yes, my dear! I'd swear to it on my dear husband's grave! Them stones were 'alive'! Well, I just looked on in amazement, my mouth wide open. It was then that they must have really sensed my presence. Stopping, they turned to face me. Suddenly, an icy chill came upon me, freezing my bones to the marrow. I couldn't stop my teeth from chattering!" Mrs Eelbake takes a deep breath, the telling bringing a renewed fear to her face. "But it was the feeling!" She begins to sob again. "The feeling… NEVER have I experienced such a feeling of pure hate and malice, in all my life! No! Never! And I'll tell you something else! I never want to experience it, ever again!"

"What happened? How did you get away?" Bill asks.

"Happened! What happened? I don't know how, but I turned my bike around and peddled for all my life was worth until I came upon your cottage. The rest, you know."

"Geez! I don't know about you lot but I could do with another cuppa?" Hannah says getting up to fill the kettle.

Bill looks out of the window. "It's gone!"

"What has?" Oswald's jostled from his thoughts.

Bill's at the kitchen door. "The mist! It's completely cleared up!"

Stepping into the garden, Oswald looks all about him. "Good Lord! You're right! How extraordinary!"

Hannah fills the teapot with boiling water. "Weird," she says, shaking her head. "Weird!"

They sip their tea in silence.

* * * *

The old analyst reads the final pages of his detective novel, with a sense of urgency and regret. Keen to confirm his suspicions that it is the thwarted mistress who is the murderer and sad that the yarn has to end. He's always enjoyed a good 'whodunit', ever since childhood, engaging this passion throughout his long life. Perhaps he'll be a detective next time around? Satisfied with the final outcome, his suspicions confirmed, he closes the book and goes to the kitchen to make himself a hot bedtime drink.

Turning on the radio, he listens to the late night news. The voice of the newsreader keeping him company, while he heats up his milk:

"And finally N.A.S.A. scientists have expressed concerns that the comet, thought to be on a collision course with Jupiter, has shifted from its expected path, and is moving closer towards Earth. Meteorologists are blaming this unexpected realignment for the erratic change in weather conditions around the world. World leaders and the scientific community issued a statement from the U.N. that there is absolutely no cause for alarm. They say the situation is being closely monitored. However, this view has been challenged by the Church of Christian Knights. Their self-styled leader, the Reverend Dick Paradise, has called upon world leaders to come clean and tell the people the truth! When pressed, by the world's media, what the truth is, he said that the world's doomed, that it's going to be destroyed by a fiery comet, and that all non-believers are going to burn in Hell."

The old analyst turns off the radio and pours his hot milk into a mug. Climbing the stairs to bed, he wonders if there's any point in setting his alarm, if the world is going to end tomorrow. Who wants to get up for that? Thinking of his analysand, he smiles and sets his clock.

* * * *

Having escorted Mrs Eelbake back to her cottage, the three companions allow themselves to be persuaded to stay for an evening meal. The three agree that they should stay with their newly acquired neighbour, until she feels safe and settled in her own home. She's still in shock and in need of some company.

 After their meal, a frugal affair, Mrs Eelbake settles them into the parlour to watch some television. Now seems a good time to take their leave. About to get up and make their excuses, their attentions is drawn to a late-night news item.

Leading politicians from all over the world have gathered at the United Nations Headquarters in New York for a conference on climate change. The President of the United States of America is being questioned by the world's press, not on the conference but rather on the comet. At his right hand side, stands the British Prime Minister, followed by the rest of the world's leaders. The British Prime Minister beams at the cameras, while the other leaders attempt half-smiles.

Hannah can't help noticing that the leading science advisors, carefully placed behind the politicians, look distinctly glum. Bill and Oswald think they look really edgy, uncomfortable and somewhat alarmed. Bill's notices that the chief scientist keeps glancing at her watch, while the others around her keep looking up into the sky, as if expecting to see something.

Having assured the assembled throng that there is no cause for alarm, and that the ongoing situation is being closely monitored, the news item cuts from the President of the U.S.A. to a fundamentalist church in the Deep South.

Outside, on the steps of his church, an exhaltant Reverend Dick Paradise calls upon the whole world to repent from their sins and wickedness, or be damned to Eternal Hell Fire. With a look of glee on his face, he slowly raises his arm, his finger pointing skyward. "It's a-coming!" he drawls. "And its got your name on it!" His finger's now pointing towards the television monitors. He smiles at all the folks at home sitting in front of their TVs as the picture fades.

The item that follows is shot outside the British Museum, where a worried-looking curator of Babylonian artefacts, tells the interviewer that the stone of Nergal had first been noticed, as missing, by a member of the general public. The stone was last positively accounted for a few weeks previously. Its disappearance is a complete mystery. The stone's a part of a collection, all more precious than it. The ancient Babylonians believed it had mysterious occult powers and was thought to be the Stone of Nergal, God of War, Famine and Disasters.

Mrs Eelbake switches channels to her favourite programme.

Taking the lead, Hannah makes her excuses, while the others follow. Showing them to the door, Mrs Eelbake thanks them for their kindness. Satisfied that she's safely locked in, the three shout their goodnights and make their way back to Crumpleberry.

Setting off towards home, the three companions link arms. A full moon casts a blue-white light over the landscape. They giggle at the shape of their three elongated shadows preceding them. In the night sky the stars shimmer and glisten. Slowly they trudge their way along the lane towards the cottage.

As they walk, they discuss the day's events. Tomorrow, they'll visit the stones. As they pass the field that houses the Whispering Knights, they find themselves quickening their step. Hannah shudders involuntarily. Bill begins to whistle. Oswald tightly grips his medicine bundle. None dare to venture a look at the stones. Not until they are safely past the field do they resume their conversation. Picking up from where they'd left off they discuss the day's extraordinary events, sharing their observations regarding the news reports.

Slipping into their own thoughts, each wonders if the news items seen have any bearings on them or why they are here. An owl hoots and they all jump. Glancing at each other, they laugh nervously. Seeing the cottage they quicken their pace.

Some Memories, Dreams and Reflections

* * * *

It's decided! They'll make an early start and visit the stones first thing in the morning. Tired and weary, they say their goodnights and make their ways to their rooms.

* * * *

Sleep comes quickly to all three, as do their dreams:

In Hannah's dream she makes her way across the fields towards the five standing stones with her two companions.

As they approach, all three notice the silence.

Strangely attracted to the Whispering Knights, Hannah walks slowly around them, peering intently into their midst, as if searching for something. Placing the palms of her hands on the stones, a cold tingling sensation hit's the pit of her stomach, plunging her into a place of awareness deep within herself.

Now she walks in an inner landscape, being drawn closer and closer towards a black pit. It both attracts and repels her. Deep within the darkness a pulsing light glows, pulling Hannah forward towards the internal precipice that lies before her. Its ruby hue calls her, willing her to come. Overcome with dread, Hannah quickly removes her hands from the stones. The sensations stop and the vision fades. She looks to her friends.

Bill's trying to avert his gaze from the Whispering Knights but their pull is strong. They're calling to him, mocking him, challenging him to face his fear, or to run, run like the coward that he is, for they know his deep, dark secret!

Feeling heavy and stuck, his secret fear insinuates itself upon his senses, creeping and crawling all over his body, making the hairs on the back of his neck stand up. Slowly, the panic wells up inside him, as the scent of death pervades his nostrils, highlighting his mortality. Bill tries to swallow but his mouth is dry.

Detached, Oswald views his two friends with interest. Isolated and apart, he wants to call out to them, but no sound will come. Struggling, he tries to find his voice, but it lies submerged, burdened down by a deep, deep, sorrow.

'What's the point? There's no hope!'

Each caged in their personal hell, they lay open the gates of despair. All seems lost!

In the depths of darkness comes light.

Its clear note comes ringing in their ears; the pristine chime of a crystal bell, followed by the faint sound of a beating drum.

Drawn away from the Whispering Knights their attention is now focussed on the circle of standing stones. Each makes their way towards them. The song of a mistle thrush fills the air, warming their hearts and lifting their spirits. Whatever it was that possessed them has now fled. Linking arms, they feel safe in each others company, as they move closer towards the circle and its protection.

It's Hannah who notices him first. She looks surprised, but Oswald and Bill greet him as a revered and respected friend. The old American Indian stands in the centre of the circle with his drum. He motions them to come forward. Nervous, Hannah takes Bill's hand. Oswald places himself opposite the old man, who's now seated on the ground. Sitting on either side, the three companions face the old Shaman Warrior.

Acknowledging each with a nod, the old shaman gazes deep into their eyes. Seeing their pure inner light shining bright within, his face displays a fleeting smile of welcome, which he replaces with a more sombre visage. Choosing his words carefully, he speaks. "The appointed time is now! You must wake from your slumbers and meet with the stones. The Great Mother has need of your medicine. You are her chosen warriors. She has need of your services, NOW! Come! Come before it is too late!"

* * * *

They wake with a start, each calling out to the other. Rushing to their bedroom doors, they open them and look at each other. Hannah is the first to blurt it out, "We're needed at the stones!" Quickly, they return to their rooms and dress.

Placing his rattle and medicine bundle in his backpack, Oswald runs out to meet Bill and Hannah, already waiting, kitted-up on their motorbike, its full lights on, its engine revving. Oswald jumps into the sidecar and they speed towards the stones, their heart's pounding in their chests. Whatever's going to happen, they're about to meet it head on! Their time has come…

* * * *

It's been a very long day:

Tired and drained, by all the sorting out, Peter and Marg fall into their comfortable bed, exhausted.

Tomorrow they'll resume their holiday. Both are asleep before their head's hit their pillows.

Needing her own space, Marg moves away from her lover's embrace and steps into her old dream:

Once more, she's a small child, lost in a fine white translucent mist, stumbling to find her way to the safety of the stone circle, whose blue and gold light crackles in the near distance. Behind her, loom five large figures, they're whispering for her to stop; turn around, see what nice things they've got for her.

Frightened by their thin voices, Marg quickens her pace. Still, the figures call out, desperate to stop her, the whine of their voices getting closer. Marg increases her speed, running as fast as her little legs will carry her. Howling with glee, the five take chase. They're closing in on her. She can hear their ragged breathing as the gap between them and her closes. Soon, they'll be upon her and then there'll be no escape! Marg can feel her panic growing. If only she can run a little faster!

The stone circle is in sight. She must get inside it! Yet, still, they're gaining! Her thumping heart is fit to burst. She can feel their breath on her neck but she won't look back, for then, all would be lost!

The knights are closing in, stalking their prey, their bloodshot eyes intent on destruction, their thin voices still pleading with her to stop. They mean no harm.

Marg refuses to listen. The circle's now within reach. If only she can keep the distance! An inner voice urges her on. Summoning her last ounce of strength, in a final surge, Marg rushes into the circle. All about her shines a brilliant blue light, golden sparks shooting from its centre. Behind her, the shadowy figures pull back. Howling and screaming they vent their rage.

Bathed by the healing light, Marg slumps to the ground exhausted, her lungs burning with pain; but she's safe! No matter how hard they might try, the five cannot enter this place, their way is barred.

Outside the circle, the shadowy figures regroup. A dull red glow pulsates within their midst, charging the area outside with an energy that exudes pure, undiluted, evil. It sparks and flares as it touches the circle of stones, but entrance is denied.

Exhausted, lying flat on her back, Marg opens her eyes and looks into the night sky. She screams in terror as a fiery burning mass hurtles out of the heavens towards her. Terrified, shaking, Marg sits bolt upright in her bed and cries out her lover's name; PETER!!!

* * * *

Sleep is a long time coming to the old analyst. Although tired, there's a nagging doubt playing in the back of his mind, telling him, there's something important he has to do. In the state between sleep and wakefulness, the old analyst feels his body gradually lightening.

Then comes a jolt, and he leaves its heavy mass behind. The ceiling's getting closer! His astral body's outside its sleeping form. It rises out of his bedroom, up through the top of the house and into the night sky.

For a while, he hovers; floating amongst the stars, surveying the scene below. Sensing the direction he needs to take, he stretches out his hands and travels out of the city, soaring over rooftops, roads and county lanes making his way towards the open fields and the circle of standing stones. But he senses tonight is different. Tonight he will not just wait. Tonight someone will come...

* * * *

Hannah pulls up in the lay-by, cutting the engine and lights. A small cloud crosses the path of the full moon blocking its light. The bright stars shimmer in the night sky, bearing witness to the three companions, as they make their way towards the field. Stopping at the gate, before they enter, they look towards the five stones. A short distance away, fenced off and tree-lined, they can just make out the large stone circle known as the Rollright Stones.

Bill addresses his companions, but Oswald's attention is distracted by a small blue flickering light, flitting about the large stone circle. Deep inside him, a faint memory stirs.

"Are you listening, Oz?"

Bill and Hannah look at him.

"Oh, I'm sorry, I'm afraid my mind wandered, could you repeat that?"

"I was saying," Bill says - a little annoyed, "that at all costs, no matter what happens, we must keep together, okay?"

Oswald nods in agreement, but there it is again, he can distinctly see it! A small blue flickering light. It's coming from the circle! Now where has he seen that before?

"Yes!" said Hannah. "And another thing, none of us should wander off the path! Is that agreed?" She looks at the other two.

"Agreed!" Bill nods.

There it is again! He's sure of it!

Hannah repeats herself. "Agreed, Oswald?"

Snapping out of it, Oswald focuses on the task in hand. "Agreed!" he mutters looking at the other two, they're obviously unaware of the light. He wonders if he should point it out.

The cloud moves away from the moon, its light casts eerie shadows from the five stones.

Bill opens the gate. "Now remember folks, no matter what happens, we've got to stick together, okay?"

Hannah nods gravely. "And we must keep to the path!"

Bill shuts the gate behind Oswald, who's last to enter the field. Bunching together, they make their way slowly towards the

Whispering Knights. A tense expectation fills the air. There's little movement, silence hanging upon the landscape, like a heavy mantle.

Out of the corner of his eye, Oswald spots it again… the blue flitting light. He stops to look closer, while the other two move on. Unaware Oswald's attention is focussed elsewhere. Surely butterflies don't come out at night, and he doesn't know any blue moths… at least, not as blue as that! Stepping off the path, he's determined to take a quick look. His companions won't notice. They're both transfixed by the Whispering Knights.

Deftly, he makes his way towards the stone circle.

Bill, sensing something's wrong, turns back to look for Oswald.

To his utter dismay Oswald's left the path and is making his way towards the stone circle. It looks like he's spotted something and is giving chase. As Bill turns towards Hannah to tell her of Oswald's diversion, a thick blanket of mist swirls towards them, covering the landscape, drastically reducing visibility, until they become mere shadows.

Hannah calls out to Bill, "Where's Oswald?"

Turning to look towards the circle Bill can only see mist. "He's gone and left the path! He was making his way towards the circle!" There's a note of panic in his voice. Peering back, Bill tries to make out Hannah's figure but all he can see is mist, even her shadow is gone. He calls out to her, "Hannah! Where are you? We must keep together!"

But Hannah does not hear! Her eyes are fixed on a dull red glow. Entranced, she follows it, its hypnotic pulse drawing her towards the five stones.

Feeling the panic rise within, Bill tries to calm himself. "Bloody marvellous! Within five minutes of entering the field, we've lost each other in this damn fog and I'm talking to myself! HANNAH!!! OZ!!!" He calls out their names but there's no reply. He's alone.

Oswald chases the pretty blue light along the field towards the fence. Unaware of his surroundings, he has all but forgotten his two companions. Stealthily, he creeps towards the blue light but just as he gets close enough to pounce, it moves off again, drawing him closer and closer towards the large circle of stones. Tingling with delight, he secretly admires the butterfly's audacity at avoiding capture, for he's sure now, that it is a butterfly. He does so want to touch its blueness!

With the stones looming larger, the blue, blue light, flits into the circle. Oswald gives chase.

Placing itself in the centre of the stones, it turns to face its would-be captor. Paws cupped, Oswald pounces and the light fades. Sitting himself up and brushing himself down Oswald feels very, very sad.

Much to her surprise, Hannah's reached the five stones, only to find that they're no such thing. The light has obviously been playing tricks on her.

Before her is a deep well. Inside it is carved flights of beautifully hewn stone stairs. Peering into the well, she can just make out the faint glow of a pulsating red light. Stepping inside, her palm firmly pressed against the side of the well wall, Hannah slowly makes her way down the flights of steps towards the glowing light. The only sound to be heard is the faint pounding of what sounds like a heartbeat. She wonders what it might be.

For a while, Bill wanders around aimlessly, calling out to his friends, receiving the same response.

Nothing!

Looking about, he tries to pick out a landmark, so as to get his bearings, but its hopeless, there are none!

This is ridiculous, he thinks, and decides to push on. If he can make it to the five stones, then perhaps, he might get his bearings? Yes! That's what he'll do. But something deep in the pit of his stomach cries out that this is precisely what he shouldn't do. So, turning about, he makes his way slowly towards what he hopes is the direction of the gate. Being an instinctual sort of fellow, its time to go with his gut feelings. Bugger the stones! He'll wait for the others at the bike! Besides, there's nothing they can do until the mist lifts. Bill thinks of poor Mrs Eelbake, out alone in the mist, and begins to realise what it must have been like for her. He feels more than a little frightened himself! But, what's there to be frightened about?

There's nothing out here that can hurt him! Is there?

Oswald checks the circle of stones for signs of the butterfly, but its nowhere to be seen. It's completely vanished.

A deep melancholy sits upon him filling him up with sadness.

Where has it gone? Why doesn't it want to be with him? Sad and dejected, Oswald makes his way to the centre of the circle and sits himself down on the ground. Large tears come to his eyes as his sadness overwhelms him. Quietly, he begins to sob, for he's afraid that people might hear, and think badly of him.

As he continues his journey, the old analyst begins to recognise the familiar landscape of his nightly travels. Now he's approaching the place of the stone circle. Soaring high in the starry night sky, he looks down upon the Earth.

Below him stand the large stones, surrounded by a thick, swirling, menacing mist.

Manically, the mist races around the circle's perimeter, desperately trying to find a way in, so that it can wreak its havoc, but its way is barred. As much as it tries, it cannot get in! Frantic and frustrated at its failed onslaughts, the mist whips itself up into an even greater frenzy, twisting, twirling, pushing, shoving, swirling, hurling itself upon its quarry, howling with frustration at not being able to get its own way!

The old man looks on with interest. The circle and its small clearing remain free of the mist. An island of sanctity and peacefulness. Calm, it radiates all that is goodness, hope and well-being. As he moves in closer, the old analyst sees the crumpled figure of a rather stout bear, quietly sobbing, his face hidden in his paws. The old man winces at the painful sight, his heart open to a fellow sufferer. The enormity of the little bear's pain is overwhelming. He seems so alone! Isolated. Cut off from the world of human kindness. It makes the old man's heart ache. He longs, to reach out and hold him, hug him, tell him that everything will be alright, that he is loved, but the old analyst knows that this is not to be his task. No, he must stand and be a witness to this poor, dejected creature. Let him sink into the depths of his despair and find his own way out. It is this; he has been brought here to do.

No longer able to gaze upon his fellow being from a great height, the old analyst chooses to level with him, meeting him on common ground, face to face. Landing quietly on the grass, he rests his back against one of the standing stones, and waits for his little friend to surface from his pain. There's no hurry.

Oswald, sensing another's presence looks up from his paws and sees the kindly old man smiling at him. Rubbing the tears from his eyes he swallows and gives a watery smile. Moving away from the stone the old man slowly makes his way to the bear.

"Hello Oswald, I've come to be with you, if that's okay?" Reaching the little bear the old man sits beside him.

"That nice," says the teddy bear, wiping his nose on the back of his paw. "I thought I was alone."

The old man takes out his big white pocket handkerchief and gives it to him. Oswald gives his nose a good blow and wipes the tears from his eyes. He looks at the old man. "I'm glad you came."

"Me too!" says the old man.

"Really?" says Oswald, looking pleasantly surprised.

"Yes, really." The old man is looking outside the circle.

Oswald feels a warm glow inside from the old man's words.

"Oswald, have you looked outside the circle?" The old analyst looks at him.

Oswald checks the old man's bow-tie. It's his favourite, the cornflower-blue. Suddenly his heart is filled with joy at the sight of it.

"What are you smiling at?" the old man enquires.

"Oh, nothing." Oswald says dreamily.

The old man looks out towards the mist.

Oswald follows his gaze. "Good heavens!" he exclaims. "Where did that come from?"

The analyst turns to the bear. "I think you know, don't you?"

Oswald looks into the mist as the scene unfolds before him. It's a bit like going to the movies, only with himself playing the leading role.

There he is! A baby elephant, standing at a water-hole in the heart of a dense jungle. Above him, seated on a tree, is a large-eyed tree frog, looking down with disapproval.

Alone, frightened, and very hungry, the baby elephant's crying, calling out for his mummy and daddy, but they do not come!

The scene changes:

It's an old Edwardian house, very large and grand, set in a landscaped garden.

Oswald cries out in recognition. "That's Ditchley Grange! I used to live there!"

Intrigued, he looks to the analyst who just nods.

"And there's Jennifer and James, the twins I used to live with! It seems nothing's changed! They're still fighting and quarrelling."

But this time it is different. Oswald looks on.

The house has been closed down and the children sent away to private schools. Oswald sees himself seated in the playroom window, there's a worried expression on his face. The argument was about him. The children were fighting over which of them owned him and who should take him when they left. Although each had outgrown him, and had paid him scant attention these past few years, both were being bloody-minded. Neither really wanted him, but they were determined that the other should not have him. This is how it had always been between them.

Now it all comes flooding back. Oswald remembers the pain and the sadness of that scene and his eyes begin to fill up with tears.

Jennifer grabs him from the windowsill, clutching him to her chest. "You shan't have him! He belongs to me!" she screams.

James tugs at his arms and ears. "He's mine! I tell you, he

belongs to me! I had him first!"

Squealing, Jennifer hits out at James, as he tugs at the bear. Kicking and pinching, hitting out with their spare arms, the two children fight over who should possess him. So ferocious is their battle that it brings the adults rushing into the playroom to see what all the commotion is about. Just as their nanny and father enter, something gives way and there is a terrible tearing sound. Oswald winces at the remembered pain. Both ears have been torn off and a large rip has been rent from his arm. Oswald howls at the pain of it. What's happening to him? Why are the children doing this?

Separating the kicking, screaming children, the two adults attempt to bring them to their senses, demanding to know what is going on!

Picking up the pieces, Nanny places the bear on the windowsill.

Unable to get any sense out of either of them, their father deems that neither shall have the bear, as neither is fit to look after it.

"Bear will remain at the Grange! Perhaps someone will come along who will appreciate him. A bear is not a possession! Why, the very thought of it!" Cross with his warring twins, he orders them to their rooms to finish their packing. Their nanny is given instructions to clear the rest of the things from the playroom and ensure that the door is kept locked. Teddy is to remain inside.

Torn and shaken, the bear lies on his side, wounded and abandoned.

Looking upon this scene, Oswald quietly weeps.

The old analyst looks at his friend, "What are you feeling?"

Oswald blows into the handkerchief as tears roll down his face. Trying to choke down his sobs Oswald tries to speak, "I…, that is…, I…feel…" he lets out a sob-torn ragged breath, "hurt…, and…, angry…"

The old man nods sympathetically and guides Oswald to look once again into the mist.

The scene has returned to the water-hole:

Disdainfully, the tree-frog looks down at the baby elephant.

"Cease that blubbing this instant! Whatever next! Fancy a large animal like you making such a silly noise!"

Angry at his parents' absence, the baby elephant begins to fill up with rage. A deep anger welling up inside him. No longer able or wanting to contain such feelings inside, the baby elephant stamps and trumpets with all his might. Furious, he picks up boulders with his trunk and throws them into the lake.

Alarmed the tree-frog tuts and shakes his head. "Well, really!" it says.

Registering the frog's disapproval in the corner of his eye, the baby elephant fills his trunk with water and lets the frog have it, FULL BLAST!!

Drenched and startled, the tree-frog flies through the air, propelled by the water from the baby elephant's trunk, landing with a thump!

Bruised, dishevelled, nursing his wounded pride, the tree-frog limps meekly into the thickets.

Appalled at his actions, yet delighted with the results, the baby elephant, laughs and laughs and laughs.

Laughing and crying at the same time, Oswald looks at the old analyst, whose moustache quivers, as he desperately tries to suppress his own laughter. Catching the mirth in each others eyes, it finally gets the better of them. Tears of laughter role down their cheeks, as they hug each other and roar with a laughter that comes deep from within. After all, what's wrong with friends sharing a good joke? Nothing!

* * * *

Whistling to keep his spirits up, Bill negotiates the mist making his way to what he hopes will be the field gate. Nothing's there! He's sure he's taken the right direction. Where is the damn thing? Now he's beginning to doubt himself. An irrational fear creeps into his mind. Slowly the panic begins to surface, he quickens his pace.

Where are the others? Why aren't I calling out their names? He shouts out their names. "Hannah! Oswald! Where are you guys? Answer me!"

He waits for a response. Nothing! But something's caught his eye. A faint red glow in the distance. At last, something tangible to follow, perhaps the tail-light of a car? The road must be close by, but why can't he hear the sound of an engine? Heartened by the thought of human contact, Bill quickens his step, making his way towards the light. As he draws closer, the dull red light gets bigger. It's pulsating. The mist surrounding it has taken on its red hue. Something's not quite right! Bill's steps falter, as he slows down and takes stock of the situation. The field's gate is nowhere in sight, which means that the light that he's been following can't be a car's tail-light! So what is it? With curiosity and caution both tugging at him, Bill continues along the track towards the red pulsating beacon. Unease permeating his whole being, his breathing becoming rapid. He listens out for noises. Nothing! All's still! Close! The blood coloured mist curls about him. Looking down at his feet, he sees the wispy strands closing about him, weaving their tendrils around his body.

Deep inside him an ancient fear cries out a warning. "Beware! Beware! For you approach death!" Bill shudders. "Geez! Somebody's just walked over my grave!" he speaks out aloud to himself, sure that no-one can hear, but in need of the comfort brought by the sound of a voice. He cocks his head and listens. "Nah! It can't be?" he's sure he's heard the rustle of skin on skin, a bit like something rubbing up against itself. His fear's beginning to get the better of him! "Keep calm!" he says to himself. His imagination is beginning to run away with him. Of course he didn't hear the sound of the duck-bill platypus' oldest enemy. "Take deep breaths!" he tells himself. "That's what you need to do, take deep breaths and calm yerself down." Breathing deeply his fear begins to subside. His rapid heartbeat slows. Just a few more steps and he'll be able to get a better view of what's giving off the light. It's situated in the centre of a sort of table construction made up of five large flat stones, placed one upon the other. It looks a bit like an altar.

More settled now, Bill moves forward cautiously. Then he hears it; a quiet hissing sound. Yes, he's sure of it, the sound of the platypus' most deadly enemy, coming from behind the altar! He stops in his tracks, deadly still, and listens for a second time. Nothing!

Now, a mere six feet away from the stones, Bill's eyes lock onto the red pulsating light at their centre. Moving closer, to get a better look, he's amazed at its small size. Approaching the altar, he reaches out to touch it.

Nergal exhales a breath of deep satisfaction and welcomes its prey. Before Bill can touch the light a large deadly fanged serpent springs up from behind the altar, striking at the platypus, with its long forked tongue. Catching the apparition in his peripheral vision, Bill jerks back, terror-stricken he screams.

He remembers his dream in Oswald's den. His worst nightmare has come to life and is here, alive, towering above him, rocking its large uncoiled body - from side to side - its small dark eyes transfixed upon him!

Rigid with fear, Bill faces the instrument of his death, his stifled screams struggling to get out. His time has come! The Great

Unspoken Fear…

Waiting for the serpent to strike, Bill becomes inwardly resigned to his fate. Mortality is staring him straight in the face, in the form of his greatest fear.

Resigned, through acceptance, a calmness falls upon him, unclouding his mind, releasing his fear. The words of his Great Uncle Billy come to him. "Don't be afraid of death Bill, for there is nothing to fear. Death is just the closing of one door and the opening of another."

Meeting the serpent's gaze, Bill waits for death to strike.

He's no longer afraid.

* * * *

Step by step, Hannah makes her way down into the well, touching the surface of the walls, with the palms of her hands. There are five flights of stairs and many steps.

As she slowly makes her way downwards, the intensity of the light increases. The feeling's strange; it's a bit like climbing down into oneself. She giggles nervously and wonders what would happen if she were to fall? She thinks of Alice, but there are no white rabbits here! Hannah peers down at the dull red light, a little fearful of what she might meet. The throbbing sound fills her ears. It's getting louder, its beat in sync with the pulse of the light.

How odd! With each flight of steps descended, the worry inside her grows. Feelings of self-hate and loathing creep from under their covers and the old nagging voice returns. BAD! EVIL! ROTTEN INSIDE! NO GOOD!

Hannah wrinkles her nose up, as the stench of her self-loathing permeates her nostrils. Perhaps it would be better for all concerned if she ended it all here? She could throw herself off the steps! She'd break her neck for sure! Nobody would miss her and it would stop the ugly feeling inside! Why must she feel so wretched? At times like this she really hated herself.

Another flight descended!

She turns to face the next. The light is much brighter now. Just another flight after this one and she'll be there. Her mood darkens. She feels frightened.

Hannah clutches at the stones. Below her, she can see a hovering black form. It's waiting for her. She cries out in panic. Tears roll down her cheeks but still she presses on, for there is no going back now. Making her lonely descent, fear wracks her body. Her tears flow freely, her shoulders shaking with all the sobbing, but still she continues her journey, downward.

The final landing.

The fifth and last flight of stairs.

Hannah turns to face the floating figure - a wrinkled old woman. She smiles at Hannah and stares into her eyes. With fascination and terror, Hannah meets her gaze. The old woman's face is gnarled and wizened. Her eyes bore into Hannah's. And for a slight moment there is recognition. Bright and powerful, they radiate energy so great and ancient that Hannah feels that it will consume her, suck the very soul from her body. The power is awesome. Hannah thirsts for its knowledge and wisdom but not; 'no,' not its darkness!

Floating closer, the old woman takes Hannah's hand. Hannah's body jolts violently, as it surges with its own unlocked power. She screams, as its boundless energy courses through every cell of her being. Orgasmic. Awesome. Its power is so great, she feels that she might explode. She craves its purity and strength but dare not accept the other!

Fixing her gaze, the old woman bursts into Hannah's soul, flying into her body through Hannah's left eye. Screaming out in agony, Hannah stumbles and falls, crashing down the last flight of stairs, her crumpled body slumped against the light.

* * * *

Exhausted by the tears and the laughter Oswald lets go of the old analyst and dries his face with his paws. The old man follows Oswald's example, using his large white handkerchief.

The scene clears, leaving only the mist. The old man notices that it is less dense, and that it is beginning to clear in places.

Filled with an inner calm, Oswald studies the old man's face and looks out towards the mist. "It's me, isn't it?"

Smiling to himself, the old man nods.

"What do I have to do?"

The old man gives a deep sigh. "What we all need to do, at some time in our life. What you have just done. Face your deepest fears, hurts, secrets, and own them, experience them."

Oswald looks up at the old man enquiringly. "Experience them?"

The old man meets his eyes. "Feel them, Oswald."

Oswald's features portrays his pain. "Yes, I see that now."

Standing up, the old man brushes himself down. "You know, I have to go now?" He points towards the figure seated by the fire. "Something tells me your company is required elsewhere."

Oswald looks towards the fire. "But why are you going, where will you go?"

"I've done what I came to do, I know that now, and my bed awaits me, but as for your journey, I think it's only partly over. My little friend, be of good courage and trust in yourself. There's more to you than meets the eye. Goodnight Oswald. May you walk in beauty, as the old shaman would say?"

The analyst and shaman acknowledge each other with a nod.

Oswald waves to the old man, as his image fades from the circle.

* * * *

Slowly, the mist is beginning to lift.

Oswald seats himself beside the fire. The shaman and bear greet each other with a smile.

It's the old Indian who speaks first. "It is good that you have come."

"What is it that I have to do?"

"You must step out of the circle and find your friends, for it is written that the Bear and the Platypus must escort the Hill Maiden to the circle with her burden."

"What's her burden?"

"Her burden's the burden of Everyman's. Her darkness, her shadow! Its manifestation, she'll know. The Great Earth Mother wishes you speed, now go!"

The image fades. The shaman has gone and the standing stones are empty save for the presence of a rather war-torn teddy bear.

Oswald picks himself up from the ground and courageously makes his way out towards the field, clutching his medicine bundle tightly in his paws. Owning his mist, he steps out into its shadows.

* * * *

There's nothing much more he can do. He'd let his wife know two days ago. She'd flown out in Air Force One to be with their daughters. They had said their goodbyes the night before. There had been some tender moments and reconciliations and they had parted as friends.

Forty-eight hours later, tired and worried, the President of the United States of America, dismisses his aides and chiefs of staff and strolls up to his private den, while they return to the crisis room. If he's needed, he can be contacted on his private line.

What he most desires now, is space to think, to prepare him for the inevitable. For once, the scientists are right! Collision is inevitable. There will be no survivors! The Earth is directly in the path of a comet that is hurtling straight towards it. Twice the size of our own planet, there is little that can be done to stop it. The comet is set to steamroller Earth out of existence. Everything that could and should have been done, has been done; and has failed. All that's left now is prayer.

The President loosens his tie and undoes his top shirt-button. Reflecting on his life, he wonders exactly what it is that he has achieved. He feels that it has been a long series of compromises, lost opportunities and broken promises. Power is certainly an addictive drug but it is also illusory. What is the point of being Mr President, the most powerful man in the world, if he can't stop a large block of ice from crashing into the planet?

Political power seems insignificant, when measured against nature.

Putting on his Ipod - a gift from his daughters - he listens to some of his favourite tracts. The vanilla ice-cream he ordered from the kitchen is on a side-table beside his favourite chair. Slumping into his chair, he puts his feet up and scoops a spoonful of ice-cream into his mouth. Looking up into the night sky, he listens to Bach, spoons and waits.

* * * *

Slowly regaining consciousness, Hannah finds herself lying on top of a hill, behind what looks like a large stone altar. She's struggling to remember what happened to her. Where's the well? And how come she's on a hill? Memories come flooding back. She remembers the old crone with her dark, dark powers. She'd entered her body and was now lodged there, sprung like a huge coiled serpent waiting to strike. She can feel the evil inside her. The serpent's sitting on top of an egg. Hannah writhes inside with self-loathing. She can't bare it, it's all too much! Feeling a sickness in the pit of her stomach, she remembers the frightening vision in the old hag's eyes. A nest of dark writhing vipers, wriggling and squirming, intent on malice, meet her gaze, their heads fashioned in the image of her own. A huge scream wells up inside her, like a volcano waiting to erupt. Hannah, wide-eyed, opens her mouth and lets out the sound. "NOOO!!! It can't be me! It can't be…!"

Her body, wracked in the agony of self- disgust, curls up into the foetal position, terror and doubt flooding her mind, as she struggles with this nightmare scenario. Is she really like his inside?

A spectre opens up before her.

The great coiled serpent, whose head bares the face of the old woman, slowly uncurls its large, shiny, scaled body and slides away from the egg. Amber in colour, the egg's the size of a small stone. From its centre pulses a dull red glow. Hannah looks on in fascination, as the egg begins to crack. From out of their shell slither two young vipers, one white the other black.

Rising up, they face each other as their bodies entwine.

The sudden sound is unexpected, causing Hannah alarm. Her heart freezes. She can hear the sound of a young child crying. Her eyes are drawn to the sound coming from the altar. A little golden-haired girl is seated there, she reminds Hannah of her daughter, Willow, aged three.

Spotting the snakes, the child climbs down from the altar and on wobbly legs makes her way towards them.

Unable to move, her heart in her mouth, Hannah looks on helpless, as the little girl gets closer to the vipers. Sensing her presence, they slowly part and slither towards her. Clapping her hands with glee, the little girl laughs, as the two snakes approach. Hannah looks on in horror. She tries to call out to the little waif -shout out a warning - but nothing will come out!

Now unsteady on her feet, the toddler falls on her bottom. Baring its needle sharp fangs, its little red tongue flicking from side to side, the white snake rapidly zigzags its way towards her. The golden-haired child reaches out to touch it, as the snake rises up to strike!

Hot tears roll down Hannah's face, as she watches the scene unfold.

Rising to its full height, the white snake poises to strike, its razor fangs, glistening in the light.

Striking out, without warning, the black snake makes its move; in a flash it bites the white snake's tail. Recoiling in shock, the white snake strikes back, biting the tail of the black snake.

Slowly, the two creatures consume each other until nothing is left but the amber stone. The image of the small child fades and the spectre is no more.

Crying and shaking with relief, calm descends upon Hannah.

Once again the old woman stands before her, a smile on her ancient face, a Crone no more. Wisdom and beauty fill her being.

Hannah looks into her eyes and can see only love, a love so pure that it warms the very depths of her soul. A love that brings with its radiance, a realisation. The realisation of the connectedness and sacredness of all things. Hannah clasps the old woman's hands in gratitude. Now, she understands. She's been given the gift of knowledge, a knowledge, which transcends the self. The old woman places the amber stone into Hannah's hand, smiles and shuffles away. No words are spoken; Hannah knows what must be done. Yawning, she stretches; and at ease in her body for the first time, Hannah lying down, falls into a deep dreamless sleep.

* * * *

Oswald Theodore Threadbare walks purposefully towards the Whispering Knights sure that he will find his friends there. As he stumps across the field, the white mist begins to rapidly lift. Now only a few hundred yards away from the stones, Oswald can make out the outlines of his two companions.

Some Memories, Dreams and Reflections

Bill's standing wide-eyed, transfixed before the stones, while Hannah lies curled up at his feet, in a deep sleep.

Heartened by the sight of his two friends, Oswald calls out to them. "Bill! Hannah! Don't worry, I'm coming!"

The two figures stir, as the distant sound of an old familiar voice resonates in their ears. Reaching his two companions, Oswald quickly assesses the situation. Sorting through his backpack he finds a small bottle of Bach Rescue Remedy. Using the dropper, he places several drops of the liquid on Bill's tongue. Taking a deep breath, Bill's body shudders, as he falls out of his trance. Although shaken, Bill feels as if a great burden has been lifted from his shoulders. Turning to Oz, he hugs him and cries on his shoulder. "Geez man, I love you!"

Oz pats him on the back, pleased with Bill's spontaneous outburst of emotion. "I know you do Bill, and I love you too. You're a dear friend." After several shared pats on the back and hugs, they let each other go.

Bill, more his old self, looks at Oswald quizzically. "Where'd you go Oz? You'll never guess what I've been through!"

Giving him another quick hug, Oswald smiles. "I think I might, but we haven't got time for that now, we have to save the planet! We need to rouse Hannah!"

Taking his rattle and smudge stick from his backpack the two of them set about their tasks.

Oswald rattles over Hannah's sleeping body, while Bill smudges her. Oswald smoothes Hannah's aura, while Bill purifies it; cleansing it from all its negativity. As they work, they chant, calling back Hannah's fragmented soul.

Stirring, as if from a deep slumber, Hannah opens her eyes and stretches. Relieved at the sight of her two companions Hannah's face breaks into a big grin. Remembering the old woman's gift, she opens her hand. The amber stone lies in her palm. It wasn't a dream, it really did happen!

Bill and Oswald help her to her feet.

"What will we do with it?" Hannah shows them the stone.

Taking her arm, Oswald turns away from the Whispering Knights and quickly makes his way towards the circle of standing stones." Come on! We must be quick! There's no time to lose!"

The full moon is on its descent. Soon it will be gone. Then will come the darkness before the dawn.

Hannah sensing the urgency of the task before them, begins to run, dragging her stout companion with her, Oswald's stubby legs barely touching the ground. They race towards the circle of standing stones, Bill following close behind!

A blood chilling scream comes from the Knights, as the three companions quicken their pace.

* * * *

Out in space the comet begins to waver.

* * * *

Heart's pounding, out of breath, the three reach the circle. In the centre stands the old American Indian. "You came!" he says. Raising his hand, Hannah places the amber stone on his palm. Pleased with their offering, the Shaman motions them to stand back.

Moving to the centre of the sacred circle, he places the stone on the ground and sits before it. Within seconds, he has placed himself in a trance, eyes closed, he begins to chant. As he does the whole ground begins to hum as a brilliant blue light seeps up through the stones, gold and silver flecks coursing through and around the circle.

Huddled together, the three companions look on in open-mouthed amazement, as the scene unfolds before them.

The Shaman - bathed in a circle of brilliant white light - eyes still closed, chants the ancient song of power. Although they cannot understand the words, the three onlookers sense their power and meaning.

Now, the stone begins to grow in size, raw-red-angry sparks issuing from its surface. Throbbing and shaking, it begins to build up heat.

The three companions step back.

Something's got to give!

Blue, gold and silver lights swirl and course around the circle of standing stones. The earth crackling with the sound of high energy.

At its inception, the explosion shakes the ground.

A bouquet of bright multi-coloured lights; erupt from the centre of the circle, propelling the Stone of Nergal into the night sky; towards the heavens!

Exploding in space; huge tremors bombard the comet with shock waves, pushing it back onto its old course.

At the same time, a mantle of rainbow light encircles planet Earth - shielding it from the explosion.

The stone circle sparks, blue and gold, and, in a final surge of blinding, healing light, its mysterious energy, fades back into the night.

Their mission is over.

The planet is saved!

* * * *

Lord Itsmyne looks on in horror as the events unfold before him. He calls for his personal assistant.

Pulling his silver revolver out of his desk drawer, he waits.

Sharpe has failed and now he'll pay the ultimate price! He flicks the switch of his precious toy from 'lighter' to 'gun'; but nobody comes.

He calls his secretary, "Where's Sharpe?"

A disinterested voice comes back from the other line, "I'm afraid he rang a few moments ago from the airport. He's resigned. He said he's going on a pilgrimage sir, to find himself, and will not be coming back."

"WHAT!!!"

Besides himself with rage, Lord Itsmyne jumps up from his desk. With anger coursing through every cell of his being, he squeezes the trigger of his gun accidentally shooting himself in the foot! Wracked in pain, and exploding with fury, he hops around his office howling and bringing down curses.

His secretary calls for the medics.

They carry him out on a stretcher.

* * * *

Tired and happy, the three companions pull up outside the cottage.

The moon has completed its cycle, and the sun is rising to greet a new day.

The joyful sound of a song thrush fills the morning air.

As the three make their way up the garden path, Peter and Marg are there to greet them, concern and relief etched upon their faces. They've prepared a breakfast fit for heroes.

For that is what they are.

Hannah has met her darkest dreams and survived.

Bill's reflected on his mortality and mastered his fear.

Oswald has allowed himself to feel, and now remembers his past.

Each has a tale to tell.

And in its telling will come an understanding.

For now though, they are content with their companionship.

Oswald thinks about his analyst.

The old man has helped him face, and revisit, his hidden past.

In doing so, it's freed him up to feel the feelings he's needed to feel.

In the reliving and the experiencing of these feelings, Oswald is aware of a new freedom. His past is now accessible.

He's ventured inside the mist and faced his shadows.

No longer does he carry the deep sense of sadness, isolation, emptiness and loneliness: all constant companions of his past.

His early years are a fog no more. His amnesia is gone.

Surrounded by his friends, he feels safe, seen and loved.

Peter looks at his old friend. "You seem different, Oz?"

"I am," says Oswald.

"I'm just glad we're out of the fog," says Bill.

"So am I," says Oswald. "So am I."

In the fields, the wildlife ventures out once more.

Placing their arms around Hannah's waist the companions make their way into the cottage.

Bill looks at his friends, "I don't know about you, but I'm starving!"

Hannah; smiling, pinches their bums.

Startled, Oswald and Bill, look at each other surprised.

Hannah gives a raucous laugh.

It's going to be another fine day.

Some Memories, Dreams and Reflections

Milton Keynes UK
Ingram Content Group UK Ltd.
UKHW021821111023
430419UK00013B/727